BUTTERFLY IN THE WIND

LAKSHMI PERSAUD

BUTTERFLY IN THE WIND

PEEPAL TREE

First published in Great Britain in 1990
Peepal Tree Press
17 King's Avenue
Leeds LS6 1QS
England

Fifth printing 2007

ISBN 0 948833 36 X

For my mother Mahadaya Seeterram

PART ONE

SIMPLE JOYS

SIMPLE JOYS

Whenever it rained I would stand and stare at the moving, dancing energy outside, and wish I was part of it. My time came. Our big yard was surrounded by tall brick walls. On this day, it became darker and cooler and lightning flashed.

Thunder rolled.

And then it came upon the rooftops, falling like a harvest of rice grains, and the wind like a sea serpent swished and curved and changed direction. Again the thunder rolled and the pounding began. The falling water bathed the shop and the gallery where I stood, and the kitchen and the open clothes-shed. An onion box, an old saucepan and two buckets in the yard were bathing. Everything was bathing.

I looked around. There was no one. My thin feet were excited but I waited.

I waited for the waterfalls and they came as I knew they would, galvanised from the roofs on to the spouting. Our roofs were many, standing at different heights, fringed with gutters and spouts. I took my clothes off and ran out to embrace the falling, dancing sprays. I was full of laughter; was thrilled and excited, for our private yard had become one gigantic shower – an emperor's luxury.

Into the middle of the waterfall I jumped, close to our green parrot and he, squawking loudly, stepped away from my splashes.

My head was pounded by the hammering water, so I offered my shoulders instead; ah, that was better!

A frog was squatting there, just gazing, pretending not to look. Was this a prince in frog's clothing? I looked at his muddy legs and then moved my hands about. He plop-plopped into the hibiscus hedge.

9

Concrete drains surrounded our house channelling the water that gushed from the spouts. I placed in them paper ships, leaves, grass, matchsticks and a boat my mother made from a single blade of Parana grass and was thrilled at the speed they all swerved, turned and sped along.

The hens were sitting under the clothes-shed, feathers close, heads bowed. Lion, our dog, slept curled like a snail's shell. Nothing stirred; but I was jumping and running wild. I dug deep into the mud with my hands and made pools and canals. The roar of the tropical downpour was all I could hear.

I looked about; the yard was now filled with shallow lakes of yellow water. Spiked saucers and crowns were dancing on the smooth concrete below. They had come from the funnels of the galvanized roof sheets, falling from a great height, bouncing their short lives away.

There were bubbles sailing away like domed ships in a vast ocean. Everywhere there were circles, ever widening, ever moving outwards, newly formed revolving circles.

Then through the rain I heard my mother call, 'Come out at once.' She walked to the kitchen and told Daya firmly to look after me, and returned to the shop.

Daya dried me and grumbled all the while, saying that I was an 'own way' child; that as soon as she turned her back I got into trouble and got her into trouble too. I could see she had been having an afternoon nap and so promised to lie in the hammock and 'behave good'.

The rains came to an abrupt end but the water in the large canal under the railway bridge and in front of our shop continued to roar.

Then a bird flew down from our zabocca tree into the yard and dipped her beak and head in a pond, as though washing her face and drying herself. Then a dip and a shake and a dip and a shake and I, watching from the verandah, began to feel pleasant and warm under flannelette sheets and more and more sleepy; thinking of a time when I was gently placed in warm water:

It is the dry season; the large white enamel basin is filled with tepid water. She has placed it in the middle of the red yard in the path of hens and ducks and our two dogs, Lion and Puppy. I am gently lowered. The old lady called Sultan mother (she lives next door and helps my mother, who is in the shop) splashes the water around me, tickles me and goes goo goo goo. Not knowing how I should respond I keep quiet.

I am soaped the same way she does Puppy, who plays with me but who can walk and run and eat faster than I. As I am feeling more comfortable, I too join in and go goo goo goo and splash the water about with my feet and hands. She soaps my head, turns me over and I am thoroughly done: beneath my chin, under my arms, between my legs, my bottom, my ears and nose. She does my neck too roughly: I am almost choking at times, but she has her own way and will not change, despite my protests.

One of her thumbs is as large as a ball and I am not happy when she washes my face, but what can I say? She says, 'There there, there, it's all over, all over,' and envelops me in a comforting dry towel. I am kissed and tickled and powdered and fed and put away. 'There is work to be done,' she whispers.

And so it is only in the evening when the sun peeps and blinks through the fine leaves of the samaan tree near the road junction, when even my shadow looks impressive, that my massage begins. My grandmother undresses me in a matter of fact way, as if she were plucking the feathers of a chicken. She puts me to lie on her outstretched feet which are my bed boards, then cups her left hand and pours out a measure of coconut oil. I feel it on my head. She tells me this is my soft centre and it needs particular care. I am now sitting on her two outstretched feet and she over-energetically massages every section of my head.

All the women, my mother, my grandmother and Sultan mother squeeze so much of their energy into me that I am sure I will grow. With the palm of her hands and fingers and with soft words, my grandmother coaxes my head to absorb the oil. She murmurs she is feeling for bumps and hollows and later says my head is well shaped; not elongated, but round and strong like the sun, a good shape. I am pleased and stay quite content. She puts me to lie at right angles across her legs, pours out another measure of coconut oil into the palm of her soft worn hands and with swift movements, completely covers my entire face, neck, and all of me with a fine film, before I can think of anything.

She pulls and releases my arms and legs, crosses and uncrosses them in every combination: right arm with left leg, both legs together, feet touching my forehead. You would think I was but a piece of dough! Noses come in for particular attention. Both thumbs are used to increase the height of the nose bridge. My grandmother reshapes every part of me to her liking.

Still holding me she stands up with some difficulty and then throws me in the air as if I were rice and catches me several times and kisses my tummy and thighs with her entire warm soft face. All this is very pleasurable and I am chuckling with delight.

Later, much later, when I was well shaped by age four, it was my turn to be the masseuse and my grandmother welcomed this change of roles.

I had to hold on to our four-poster bed to keep my balance as I massaged her back by walking up and down and up and down. There were parts of her shoulders I had to stand still on, and press down hard, because it helped to ease her pains. After this I massaged in the mustard role and then walked up and down her now slippery, hot back. This mustard role was as innocent-looking as Vaseline but as vicious as glowing charcoal on your skin. The palms of my hands and the soles of my feet became as hot as black clothes-irons on lighted coal-pots. My grandmother's skin had changed colour in parts but remained soft. It had lost its elasticity and was such a contrast to my own that I found it difficult to believe that one day I too would be covered by skin that had lost its firmness.

'It was full moon, bright full moon,' my grandmother said, 'make no mistake about that, and after ten years, ten years without the cry of children in the house, to keep us young and strong and bring us blessings...' She paused and I could hear the silence and the bouncing fall of the peas we were shelling in the large enamel bowl. '"A girl child," I heard the midwife say. A Monday it was, full moon. Bright full moon. I tell you. Look, you see right down to the clothes shed? It was as clear as day, on the night you were born.'

I didn't understand why bright moonlight at the hour of birth was important, but because older people behaved as if it was, I too, with time, felt its significance.

My parents said I was a lucky child. Nothing had happened to make me feel so, but when my father's eldest sister, his *didi,* told me, 'You must come and buy something in my shop one of these days. Don't forget now! You must be the first person to enter the shop that morning,' I felt both uncomfortable and important. Important that I should be carrying some invisible source of good luck; but ill at ease, lest this experiment prove the contrary and I lose my reputation. Fortunately my aunt, seeing my reluctance, never did press me, and I was greatly relieved for I did not believe I had the power to increase her takings for the day. Nevertheless, there was a strong belief that some people were luckier than others.

Once I heard my father say that every human being brought with him his own luck at birth, which stayed with him always like his shadow. So, whether he married or went abroad, he took his luck with him. Not unnaturally I wanted to know what luck I had brought with me, especially as I was so long in coming, born ten years after my brother and at an hour when the moon shone so brightly that the entire length of our large yard was clearly seen.

Before my birth, my parents and my elder sister and brother lived behind the goods shop. With my birth came a period of expansion: the shop grew in size and my parents were able to add three substantial rooms, a gallery, a dining room, a drawing room and a large kitchen to their domestic comforts. My mother believed in large kitchens; she said she wanted to be able to move about freely on the days she catered for as many as a hundred guests, as at a *katha*.

But that was not all. My father had simultaneously negotiated the purchase of a prime piece of property on the Tunapuna Eastern Main Road. It was a corner plot at a busy and important junction which became busier and more important and more valuable with time. Many years later my mother referred to this property as the family's 'gold'.

It was difficult for me to understand how my presence brought about all this good fortune, considering I could hardly spell. Besides, my confidence in myself wavered when my sister Maya (and I do not now believe a word of this) pointed out several times to friends and family, that I had been reluctant to learn to walk; that I had been happy to creep about in the yard with the ducks and chickens for far longer than was necessary. She would also tell people that I would shuffle down the few steps into the yard by moving backwards, using my bottom as an aid, in a way not seen before nor since. She would even show how I accomplished this, and while everyone present laughed until they cried, I was sure I never possessed such ungainly movements.

Later my brother Rajiv and my sister Kavita were born, though according to the pundit neither of them was as lucky as I. My main rival was yet to come; he was the last member of our family, my brother Arjun. His luck, the pundit said, was bountiful and surpassed even my own.

This news did not disturb me for it was difficult to be jealous of someone newly born, who was helpless and could not read or write or spell. And when he grew so did I; I was pleased to discover this would always be so.

For this reason it was I who was chosen by my mother to accompany her at nights to the religious cinema shows, as well as to Port of Spain, the capital, on shopping expeditions. This latter always included an enormous glass of ice cream sundae followed by delicious flaky Danish pastry filled with warm cherry jelly. To have all this sitting on a high stool, looking at the fresh cream cakes in the glass case between mouthfuls, inhaling the rich flavours of my favourite ice creams – coconut and soursop as well as the warm sweetness of spiced syrup – was a heavenly delight.

All this I kept to myself and in particular did not tell my brother Arjun (though he with other members of my family enjoyed the bag of cakes and pastries my mother always brought home). But when I sat in the shop, short legs dangling, my mouth full of so much goodness, I dared to wonder whether the pundit had made an error.

But whether it had to do with my 'luck' or not, by the time I was sent to primary school my parents were considered well off both by the standard of our village and by our town, Tunapuna, over the railway line, where my father had opened a brand new rum shop.

PRIMARY SCHOOL

My mother believed in education in the same way some people believe in God – the earlier the introduction takes place, the better. And so it was one morning at the age of three and a half, and without any forewarning, I was taken by the hand and handed over to a slim lady whom my mother called Miss Medina, but whom everyone else called 'Miss'.

'I have brought Kamla, Miss Medina,' she said.

Seeing Miss Medina occupied, my mother wasted no time (waste of any sort she deplored). 'I see you're busy so I will leave her right here in your charge.'

'That's alright, Mrs. Maharaj, I have got her particulars somewhere here,' Miss Medina replied, searching for something on her crowded desk.

The Tunapuna Government school had a fence of red galvanised sheeting and was separated from our shop by the

15

railway line, the railway embankments, the open drain and the unpaved reddish yellow road. Thus I could see little of the school even when I climbed on to the shop counter with the help of a high stool. But many children going to that school passed the shop each morning so I was not surprised that I too was now attending there.

I was not sent to the Canadian Mission (C.M.) Presbyterian school where my elder brother and sister had been. Many of the village children went there, but it meant crossing the ever busier Eastern Main Road. Though I had to cross the busy railway line, old Bhaktin the gatekeeper had been told to keep an eye out for me, and I knew she would shut the gates when a train was approaching so I had nothing to fear.

I was not long in discovering that Miss Medina owned everything, even the classroom. Several times each day she would say:

'I will not have my classroom looking like a pigsty,' or 'I will not have all that hubbub coming from my class.' Although I had not seen a pigsty nor knew what a hubbub was, I could tell they were not pleasing things. It was not so much knowing what words meant, but how they sounded when Miss used them.

There were other times when I believed Miss Medina thought that we were her children. I once heard her saying loudly to the young teacher next door, 'My children, these little ones, simply cannot concentrate with all that noise coming through from your class.'

But there were some things Miss Medina liked. One thing especially: straight lines. On a morning, when we were all seated on our low benches and just before we started work on our bright red and yellow abacus, her very first command would be, 'Keep in line please.' Keep in line meant making sure that the four legs of both your table and chair fell neatly within her chalk mark, an open square drawn on the floor.

It pleased her greatly when we sat straight, stood straight and left and entered the class room in straight lines. I once thought of giving her sweets wrapped in a page full of neat straight lines of different colours for her birthday.

We got along well with her because, unlike our parents, she liked doing the very things we did; the main difference being that while she used yellow, red and blue crayons on the walls and on the green movable partitions, we were given drawing paper to do the same. We played with Plasticine and so did she. Her Plasticine work was left on benches and tables for inspectors to see, while we had to squash ours up, no matter how hard we tried.

Two days before the inspector came, we did our very best tidying up our class room, washing our slates under the tap and drying each by swinging it in the air. Our neat exercise books – with a red pencil margin drawn by Miss Medina – were brought out from the closed cupboards and we had to copy out short words in our best hand. We were told to be particularly quiet when he was near by and neat in our appearance.

When the inspector arrived he spent most of his time with Miss Medina. I think he liked her. When I told Lucy who sat next to me that he was not inspecting *us,* she said, 'Grown ups are like that.'

Paperwork period was a busy time. The small scissors had to be distributed along with the glue, brushes and damp rags. Spider's web was my favourite, especially on days we were given cheerful, smooth, glossy paper, yellow and red. We were also taught to make such things as picture-frames, envelopes, cubes, hats, boats and boxes.

Although I liked cutting out pictures from old magazines and letting them tell a story, I also enjoyed using the abacus. The beads slid smoothly along your fingers and you could make sure you got everything right by doing it a second time. I discovered too how to make sure that my subtraction was correct. It was such an exciting discovery.

Compared to the abacus, which was predictable and made sense, I found nursery rhymes quite contrary. Take Humpty Dumpty for example: Well! Imagine sitting on a wall! If my mother had been Humpty Dumpty's mother, he would have been better trained and would never even have thought of sitting on a wall.

And there was the Gingerbread man. When the fox's jaw went snap as Miss Medina's did when she told us that story, I could see he should have walked along the dark tunnel of the fox's tummy and tickled it, so that the fox would laugh and laugh and laugh and out he would come. When I put my hands up and said so, Miss Medina told me, not very kindly, to sit down and keep quiet. Many years later I learnt that a man called Jonah did just that, when he was inside a whale.

However, the four and twenty black birds who were able to sing after being baked in a pie did make sense to me because my mother had told me a story of a cat and her kittens who unknown to anyone had fallen asleep in a well-prepared, full kiln. When the humble potters discovered that the meowing sounds were coming from within their now fiery kiln, the entire family prayed and prayed all day and all night. Days later when the kiln had cooled and its door opened, the pots were beautifully and evenly baked and the cat and her kittens walked out unsinged.

Nor did I have any difficulty with the cow jumping over the moon, because my grandmother had told me that the god Hanuman, when a mere child, had mistaken the moon for an attractive berry and had swallowed it. He had to be coaxed to give it up. I witnessed this myself in a film. The earth became quite dark while Hanuman kept it in his mouth. Surely, I reasoned, if the moon can be kept in one's mouth, a cow can jump over it.

But I was worried about the poor maid whose nose was picked out by a blackbird; just to make sure that our maid would be on her guard when she saw a blackbird approaching, I recited the rhyme to her slowly and clearly, but she made little of my warning.

I had meant to ask Miss Medina, why was Jack wearing a crown? Surely no one in our village would give a child a crown to wear if he were merely going to the standpipe to fetch water.

But I did not discuss this and many other things with Miss Medina, because she did not encourage us. She would simply say, 'Sit down and keep quiet; you tire me out.' Lucy said she was getting old as she already had two grey hairs above her left eyebrows. I wondered if she was taking milk daily. I did. My mother said milk was good, though I did not like it. I thought it was meant only for baby cows but kept that to myself.

The years rolled on. I left Miss Medina's class and moved up the school. I had thought then that I was leaving nursery rhymes and dark tales of wolves, witches, stepmothers and dragons behind; but as I progressed I discovered that in history books were tales of far darker iniquity.

THE BROOK

Deep in the long grass, there is a small brook. It flows beside the gatekeeper's thatched house. Old Bhaktin knows I go there and have been going for a long time, but no-one else does. I take a few sweet Marie biscuits from the round black tin barrel in the shop, and while I nibble on the bank, the tiny fishes in the brook nibble too at the grass and water weeds.

The brook is clear, I can see every pebble and gravel on its soft bed. Often I would empty my pockets and give the fish the crumbs, but the moment I step into the brook, no matter how carefully, they all disappear. I cannot tell where they go, so there must be safe hideaway places under the overhanging ledge.

I have tried talking to them and though they would look at me and move their mouths freely, I cannot tell whether they are drinking water or talking. It must be very difficult to speak under water.

There is a rusty iron funnel projecting from the damp light brown earth and from there the water pours. Bhaktin says that it comes from Mount St. Benedict, passes behind my grandmother's house in St. John's Village and runs under the town to appear in her back garden.

I tried catching the fish with my cupped hands but they were too quick and slippery. So one day I left an empty guava

19

jam jar on the bed and went away. The next day I returned but there was no fish. Once there were two fishes but as I tried to get them, they flowed out of the jar just as I stepped into the brook. I decided then to attach a piece of string round the mouth of the jar so that I could lift it gently without entering the water. This worked. I caught one fish and took it home and showed everyone but no one was as delighted as I. My mother said, 'What will you do with it? Put it back.'

But had I not tried hard to get one into the jar? How could I just throw it back after all that effort? So I left it in the jar and wished it good night. In the morning I saw that someone, perhaps our dog, had knocked the jar over. The fish lay still. It was limp. And when I put it back into a jar of fresh water, it did not awaken. I shook the bottle. It stayed at the bottom. It did not move.

Daya said that I had to get rid of it or it would make the whole place smell. I dug a hole and buried it in the garden and placed a stone to mark its burial place as grown ups do. I was sad and felt that I had taken its energy, its strength. I never captured another, but continued to visit the clear brook and would listen to its song and talk to the fishes. I told them my fears about school and they listened. 'What do you think of what I have said?' I would ask. And they would echo, 'What do you think? What do you think? What do you think?'

MY GRANDMOTHER

I was very close to my grandmother and she used to let me comb her long greying hair. I busied myself in making her attractive and would curl her fine soft strands into a bun, cheekily to the side, or like an empress on the crown, but never at the back, for that was far too commonplace. With the help of a pony tail or two plaits with bows at the end, she became a schoolgirl.

When I was through with hairdressing, I would count all the silver bracelets she wore, from her upper arm to her wrist. There must have been about twenty-one on each arm. (She had gold bracelets too, but kept these for weddings and visits to her mother.) I would try them on, but on me they looked more like a string of earrings hanging from a slender rod. As my grandmother got older, she wore only those from her elbows to her wrist. And as I grew taller and taller, she wore fewer and fewer until she carried only one bracelet on each arm. 'You need strength to wear bracelets,' she once remarked.

I learnt a lot from and about my grandmother by observing how she made soup; planted yams, cassava, and spinach; or made home- grown, home-ground coffee and cocoa from her ripened beans.

A decision to make a soup was not taken lightly. A soup would only be decided upon if she noticed there was a supply of good quality vegetables. Then Daya would be told which coconut to grate from the dozen or so dry ones kept in the old shed. Red beans, black-eye peas or freshly picked and shelled pigeon peas formed the main base of her soup. She chose all her ingredients with the eye of an old warrior choosing young men to defend a crucial gate.

Cassava, red sweet potatoes, coconut milk, a few spinach leaves, and the long succulent bodi beans, cornmeal dumplings, chicken or salt fish, sweet peppers, two hot bird-peppers – one yellow and one red – chives, garden herbs collectively referred to as 'seasoning' and a tablespoon of red Norwegian butter were added. As the smoke from the wood-fire embraced the huge pot, she narrowed her eyes and stirred slowly. That soup was delicious. She knew it and expected you to say so.

When she was about to harvest the cacao beans she would first gather her grandchildren together in her cool shady garden with its coconut, pomerac, chennet, pawpaw and several mango trees and we would help her cut open those beautiful red, yellow, orange and deep purple cacao pods. I loved cacao trees for they were the only trees from which a child (even one only two feet tall) could pick fruits without tiptoeing. She allowed us to suck the soft white sweet meat covering the ripe beans on condition we did not lose them. The beans were stored in boxes to ferment for several days, then spread out on galvanized sheets for drying in the hot sun. Many days later they were parched, their outer covering removed and finally ground in a mill. What came out looked like a soft, very thick, dark brown chocolate cake mixture. To her cocoa she added vanilla pods, fresh nutmeg and bay leaves and many fine things. My grandmother would then take this rich cocoa mix in her hands and roll it into a round or oblong ball, and within hours this ball became as hard as a nut. All this while the entire house was enveloped with warm chocolate and sweet vanilla smells. I remember once coming from school and knowing, sixty yards away from home, that my grandmother had come, for the length of the road was enriched with the aroma of those dark beans. She was as particular with her coffee beans and left me with the knowledge of how fine fresh coffee ought to smell and taste.

But there was another side to my grandmother, one I had not suspected, and came to quite by chance.

One day our washer-lady Renee, our cook Daya and my grandmother were shelling peas and laughing their heads off at a story my grandmother had just related. It was not meant for my ears, but in a house where all the windows and doors are open and where hens and ducks, ducklings and chicks walk in and out, the spoken word also moves freely.

My own recollection of this tale is as follows but I cannot tell it the way my grandmother did. She spun out its delicate weave with far greater skill, while I give only the bare bones:

There was a woman whose husband returned home earlier than was expected. Another gentleman, who ought not to have been there, was in the house. (At the beginning of this tale I thought the stranger must be a thief for we had thieves enter our home. As the tale unfolded I discarded this possibility.) The woman, hearing her husband coming through the door, coughing and grumbling, hid this stranger beneath her wide billowing skirt and equally wide billowing fresh cotton petticoats trimmed with fine lace. It would appear her husband did not approve of this gentleman, but my grandmother gave no reasons for so great a displeasure.

I was intrigued by this, in fact excited by such cunning, for I knew I could not have thought of such a hiding place, and this ingenuity in the face of danger I admired. Yet there remained for me many puzzling things. I wanted to know how this hidden stranger managed. I suffered from claustrophobia and other problems arose in my mind which I felt needed clarifying. So I jumped off the chair I was sitting on (my legs could not yet touch the floor), and with pencil in hand, for I had been doing my sums, approached the three women, curiosity aroused and wishing to be enlightened.

When they saw me they became hushed but still their faces were radiant with amusement. Facing them I waited.

'How would he breathe?' I blurted out.

'Who?' Renee asked, her forehead frowning and looking more puzzled than I.

'The man that is hiding,' I said; for I had unconsciously placed myself in the position of the stranger and wished to know the outcome.

'Which man?' Daya questioned with a blank face.

'How will he know whether the lady is going to move forwards or turn around?' I probed.

These three women had been enjoying a banter before I appeared, now they were behaving quite differently. In my innocence I stood my ground, but seeing that I would get no help from anyone, raised my pencil to my temple, thinking, hoping to solve this impasse. Suddenly, without warning, Renee, like an overripened mango on a tree, split open, unable to control her laughter any longer. She held on to her tummy, threw back her head and allowed all her ripe energy to ripple away in laughter. She kept pointing to me as if I were the source of this stream of enjoyment. I stood still and watched her, my eyes growing larger in consternation; every-time she looked at me she appeared to receive renewed energy for still riper ripples of laughter. 'You see this child here, she will be the death of me, I tell you,' she at last managed to say, wiping her laughing eyes. I stood and stared feeling uneasy, unhappy and embarrassed, not knowing why.

Daya got up and busied herself with dishes in the kitchen sink and my grandmother held my hands, 'You know the yams we planted?'

I nodded.

'Well come, let me show you something.'

Still holding my hands she brought me to the earth mound we had built together. It looked like the belly of a woman with child. Out of this belly of rotted kitchen compost and cow's manure had popped a slender tendril with the tiniest of leaves; so tender, yet it had emerged and now it had the courage to wave to the wind.

'Look,' she said, 'it has caught. Go bring some water.'

I brought three quarters of a bucket and while she watered it gently, sprinkling it with her hands, I thought: 'How can this clean juicy stem with leaves so well formed come out of this black earth wriggling with reddish brown worms? How can rotting things give life? How does the tendril clean itself as it struggles upwards breaking the earth's surface? How can it push itself out of that mound? Where does its strength come from? Why is it green?' But I kept all these things to myself, afraid to ask, for I was still distressed and confused at the reactions to my earlier questions.

My grandmother looked at it and said, 'It is coming on.'

I nodded.

'I am leaving you in charge. I have to go up the hill now; don't forget to water it.'

Having earlier told my mother of her plans, everything was ready for my grandmother's journey to her home, where my youngest uncle also lived. I was asked to accompany her for she had much to carry. Her clothes were washed and ironed and there was a basket with a rich Madeira cake, called plain cake to differentiate it from the very rich Caribbean fruit cake. There was sugar cake and paradise plum, a package of Huntley and Palmers biscuits, pumpkin seeds saved from a good quality pumpkin we all enjoyed and a New Hampshire cockerel, whose feet were tied together and whose wings were crossed over. He was given a drink of water before the journey and as I looked at him in the basket his defiant eyes said:

'Get me out of here, what's all this about?'

I said, 'You are going to St. John village but you're not for eating, Aji says so.'

There were also buttons and different coloured threads and cake tins requested by my aunt and an end piece from a strong flowered cotton material, suitable for a table cloth.

With a handkerchief, matches, cigarettes and a small purse in her pocket, my grandmother picked up her bags and nodded at me. I picked up mine and she called out to Renee and Daya. 'Well I'm going now, all you stay well and keep an eye on the garden for me please.'

'Not to worry and we not here?' said Daya.

'When you coming back, Mai?' Renee asked.

'I'll have to see how things stand over there.'

'Stay well then.'

'Hurry back,' shouted Daya.

'Alright then,' said my grandmother; and weighed down with gifts for her grandchildren she walked through the crooked galvanized gate out into the dusty dirt road. I followed behind. The cockerel closed his eyes.

THE CONDUCTOR AND THE BUTTERFLY

I walked up the rostrum and held my head high for the orchestra was waiting; standing before it, feeling its hushed silence, I lifted my chin and with a gentle sway of my arms as if performing some ancient magical rite, the orchestra came to life and the air was filled with sounds bewitching in their beauty and clarity. My arms expressed *spirito*, *fortissimo* and *pianissimo*. I was completely engrossed, and with the sun upon me I closed my eyes.

The piece was an enchantment.

Later, as the tensions within the music grew and grew like a mighty wave rolling on and gathering strength, my feeling of excitement and power could be contained no longer and the orchestra and I were lifted to a mighty crescendo; drums rolled and the cymbals clashed and when the ending came, the applause that greeted me was like the opening of the heavens. I stood on the rostrum. Uplifted. Alone. I bowed and bowed again; each time more deeply and slowly, like a mandarin from ancient China.

Meanwhile the sun was rising in the sky, beating down more fiercely, and my six year old skin could take no more, so I stepped down gingerly from the now much shaken rostrum of smoked herring boxes, prune boxes and blue and brown soap boxes. I ran to the standpipe in our yard and with cupped hands drank my fill, for the thirst of a six year old conductor is large. I washed my bare feet and sought rest and shade by the roots of our rose mango tree.

Only then did I throw away my green hibiscus baton. But there in the middle of my grandmother's vegetable garden still stood my ramshackle cairn of boxes. I knew I would have to remove them before she returned.

I had chosen the time and the place for this performance with care since no one I knew, well certainly not Daya nor Renee, would appreciate such a work; indeed my very stance as a conductor was completely outside their experience. 'Kamla, child,' they would say, 'you have nothing better to do than make believe? You know real good how to waste time.' But such are the limitations of grown ups.

I must be fair to them for they were both kind to me. Neither had seen the Sunday matinee show I'd seen at the Monarch cinema. In that film I was introduced to a rosy-cheeked, stout, perspiring conductor in coat-tails playing to a large crowd at a country fair. You should have seen how the old and the young ladies looked at him. I knew at once it was a role that needed a rostrum and an audience and one I would like to play.

Having rested I began to build an intricate irrigation system. My excavator was an old disused cutlass and a sharp edged stone. I rose to fetch a bucket of water to test for myself whether the law of gravity would work for me and was on my way to the pipe when, a few yards from me, I saw a beautiful lady butterfly. Like an opera fan she was, of vermillion silk, and moved her wings ever so slightly, pausing as she opened outwards, only to close them again, as if keeping time with some music I could not hear.

On each fan was a single dark eye; almost like my own I thought. She continued to sway gently in the breeze, in time with the bending, slender heads of the pigeon pea shrubs she rested on. I wanted to get closer. This called for cunning. I moved quietly away but was only pretending, hoping this would deceive her as she wafted unguardedly in the sun. Then I changed course, moving in the same way as a school compass. Creeping on all fours I drew closer and closer.

But the wind suddenly blew harder and carried her away. I was furious but patiently began to stalk her again. From my vantage point, hidden by a clump of shrubs, I could see the magnificence and the vulnerability of those gossamer silks of deep purple. She looked so delicate, yet throbbing with the magic of life and enjoying the sun beams and the nectar of all that was around her.

Suddenly as if from nowhere (could it have been from the wind? or from the God of Preservation?) a thought came to me: 'Will she fit into my cupped hands as she struggles to escape?'

Then, as if from the angry heavens, a loud shout pierced my ear drums: 'Lunch ready!' It was Daya.

Over the tops of the pigeon peas she rose, struggling against the wind, tumbling awkwardly this way and that, higher and still higher until she climbed our brick walls, rising eighteen feet high, to escape the fortified yard.

Daya pushed not only her head but her chubby top half through the window and repeated, this time in a lower octave, 'Lunch ready.'

I said nothing, still staring at the open space above the wall; thinking that she might, just might return.

'What you doing?'

'What is it?'

'Fish.'

'What kind?'

'Carite.'

'You know I don't like carite.'

(Silence)

'What else?'

'Bodi.'

'I want moonshine.'

'Boysie did not have moonshine today.'

I could hear Renee's voice. Then Daya said, 'Renee say is not the season for moonshine.'

(Silence)

'You coming?'

'I don't like carite.'

'Well you go and tell Didi. I have to cook what she gives me.'

'Carite too fresh.'

'I washed it twice with lime. Come man, it tasting good.'

My lunch was put on the table, covered with a white tea cloth and I was warned if I didn't come quickly, the cat would. I ate curried carite fish and rice with steam-fried freshly picked *bodi* garnished with home grown tomatoes; and instead of enjoying this feast, I felt that I had made a sacrifice, had done my mother and Daya a favour in eating something that was not on my list of favourite things.

RENEE

Renee had short hair, the sort of hair she said, 'You can't do nothing with', but she didn't have the time or the energy to put her hair the way she would have liked.

She and her sister Berta lived in the same wooden house separated by a wooden partition down the middle. There were two front doors and two front steps. Renee's was to the right. One of her steps was missing, so if you were not up to it, it was better to call out to her from the yard than knock at the door. The house was wearing away but Renee was so busy trying to make a living that I don't think she noticed.

Renee was our washer-lady, who kept us looking, in her own words, 'respectable'. She was very good at her work; my mother said so, and my mother was not easy to please.

I was always at ease with Renee because she had no secrets. When she began to lose her back teeth she told me, but I thought little of it. It was only when one by one she lost her front teeth and their absence could be seen (she could not afford to have make-believe ones from the dentist) that I began to feel really sorry for her, especially when she laughed, for then she showed the world the harsh disfigurement that came with poverty.

And so whenever Renee laughed and joked and showed her red gums and missing teeth I was overcome with sympathy for her and could not laugh. Renee said I could not enjoy a joke and in turn felt sorry for me. How could I tell her why I couldn't laugh? Once she told me, 'You take it from me, Kamla – and I am speaking from experience – a good belly-full of laughter is better than any medicine.'

I remember the day Renee came for the job of washer-lady. I was sitting on a high stool, 'minding the shop' while my mother was having her lunch.

'Eh! Eh! Kamla how you child?'

'I alright, Miss Renee.'

'Your mother want a washer?'

'Yes.'

'Well go and tell her I come for the job.' I went inside and returned.

'Ma said she coming just now.'

'Why you not at school?'

'I sick.'

'What wrong with you?'

'Fever.'

'You had any fever-grass tea?'

'No.'

'I will send you some fever-grass. Boil it strong with two cups of water. Then go and lie down. Wrap up well, you know, and in no time you will sweat that fever out.'

'How it does taste?'

'Good.'

'Bitter?'

'Good; real good. Besides, what you worrying about taste for? You have a fever?'

I nodded.

'Well then. You want to get rid of it?'

'No!'

'But eh! eh! Look at my crosses here. I don't believe I hearing right.'

'I don't like school.'

Before Renee could say another word my mother came through the door.

'Morning Maharajin.'

'Morning.'

'I hear you want a washer so I come for the job.'

'I don't want somebody who will come this week and sick next week.'

'I'm not like that; you can ask anybody about me. When I take a job I take a job.'

'Good. Now let me tell you this. I like my clothes to have two wash. A first wash then a rinse; then a second wash and a bleach in the sun; then a rub and a rinse.'

'I know how to wash, Maharajin. I washing clothes since I was that high.' And she showed a height of two feet above the ground.

'It is my duty to tell you how I want the clothes wash, so later, you can't say you didn't know.'

'Alright, Maharajin you win. Now how much you paying. I hope it good.'

'One more thing before we talk about pay. I like my clothes rinse clean, clean, clean. The last rinse musn't have any trace of soap. I will come now and then to examine the rinse water, so I am telling you from now. If clothes not properly rinsed, my whole skin does itch me.'

'Alright, Maharajin, but that means a lot of water.'

'I don't mind the water.'

'You have a pipe in the yard?'

'I have two pipes and two tubs. One of the pipes just above the tub, and the other, one step away.

'Well alright then. Now how much?'

'I want the clothes put out on the bleach before twelve o' clock so they will get good sun.'

'I understand all that, Maharajin. But eh! eh! When will I hear about the pay?'

'Well it is half-day work. Three half-days, no work on Wednesday; and on Friday you iron. I'll give you $10.00 a month with lunch; and breakfast too if you want it – that is left entirely to you.'

'$10.00 Na, Maharajin, I can't do all that extra rinsing for $10.00. Make it $15.00.'

'Look, you don't have to tote water. You have a shed to hang things out in case it's raining and when you hang out the clothes and leave, the cook or I will bring them in. You don't have to come back. When you leave you leave.'

'You know the price of things today, Maharajin? Prices steep steep I tell you.'

'You getting breakfast and lunch.'

'Maharajin, I have two children. How you think I will manage on that.'

'You not getting help from their father?'

'You know how it is. He doesn't have anything steady.'

'Look I making it $12.00 and you can take it or leave it.'

'Throw in two packages of cigarettes there for me na?'

'You should stop smoking.'

'You think I don't know that? You know how many times I tried?'

'Cigarettes does stifle you little by little. It does hold you like a crab. You know Daniel mother? I went to see her, night

31

before. All the time I there, she going like this "Hah ah; Hah ah; Hah ah." She can't get the air in – bad bad asthma. And you with two children too, you should know better.'

There was a long silence as if both had said all that there to say. But Renee was waiting, hoping. Then she said, 'You think I don't know they not good for me. Look at my life, Maharajin; you think if I could stop I wouldn't stop? You tell me that?'

There was another long silence and I was beginning to feel hot, sleepy and tired. My mother said, 'I shouldn't do this; it's against my better judgement, but every Monday when you start the week I will put out a package of cigarettes for you with the soap, blue and starch.'

'You are a hard woman, Maharajin.'

'Now tell me, you can start today?'

'Tomorrow. I have to sort out some things at home today if I am going to turn out tomorrow.'

'Now don't let me down. I am depending on you.'

'I will be here tomorrow, Maharajin, and thanks eh.' As she was leaving the shop she said, 'I will send some fever-grass for Kamla.'

'Fever-grass is good but you think Kamla will drink it? We will see.'

Fridays were tough days for Renee. It was ironing day and the days of black irons heated on a coal fire in a coal pot. Daya got things ready for her, the coal pot with a good steady fire and four black, smooth, well cared for irons. Renee worked very hard and ironed all our visible clothes from handkerchiefs to my father's trousers.

By four o'clock she would be finished. Then began the greasing up (as if she too were an iron) with soft candle wax – her neck, face, arms and legs and all the bits of her that showed out of her dress. Next came the 'wrapping up'. When she was finished there was little of her left. Renee was afraid of catching the 'draught', though she lived just three minutes walk from us, that is if you were to walk slowly.

But before she left she would say, 'Look here, I better take one for the road, oui.' A half bottle of Vat 19 Trinidad rum was kept in the cupboard for this purpose. Many years later when I was asked to pour someone a drink, I gave our visitor a Renee's measure, only to be told, 'What's wrong, you want to kill me?'

Having poured it out she would 'throw it back', all in one go. This too I learnt from Renee until I realised that her manner was uniquely hers and should not be copied. 'That's to keep the cold away, Kamla,' she would say. And before she finally left on a Friday afternoon, she would sit down and enjoy long pulls from a lighted cigarette. Her hands would be cupped around it and then a long slow pull. I think these were some of the more comforting moments of her short hard life. Greased, wrapped up and with Vat 19 fire in her throat, pulling at the warm nicotine, she seemed to be in a world of her own, to have opened the closed casement and allowed her spirit to soar out into the air, the trees, the clouds and the fragrance of flowers.

Seeing me looking at her with so much interest – for neither my mother nor Daya smoked or drank – she would say time and time again: 'Kamla, you listen to me now; you don't take up this bad habit, you hear me.' And I remember once saying to her, with the kind of thoughtlessness only the young can have, 'Why do you then?'

'Too old to give up now. You can't straighten an old tree. A young tree, yes. Like you, Kamla, yes. Once the sap is plentiful.'

'But you are not an old tree. Old trees don't know better, they don't have your sense.'

'But eh eh! Look at my trouble here now. You behaving like a real old lady, Kamla. Ah,' she said with sad weary eyes, 'I hope you never have these problems, Kamla, my problems'. A deep silence then enveloped her.

There was so much sadness in her that I realised at once that my glib thoughtlessness was cruel. As if reading my thoughts she said:

'Kamla dear. You can know you are doing something wrong and yet not have the strength to fight it.'

'Why don't you ask God then?' I heard myself say.

'Look here, when you grow up, don't be a magistrate you hear me. I wouldn't like to have to stand before you.'

'You are my friend, Renee. I would say, "Case dismissed" when I see it is you.' Her face lit up and she laughed. 'Well,' she said, 'that's nice, helping out your old friend Renee eh?'

'Yes,' I said.

'Case dismissed' were two words I had heard my father use frequently. From time to time he was charged by the police for selling Trinidad rum on a Sunday, a day when people who drank preferred to buy their rum. I couldn't understand why the police were upset if people wanted to purchase a bottle to drink at home on a Sunday and my father was prepared to sell it. My father soon discovered that the police were happy to allow others to drink on a Sunday if they too had a drink, so my father obliged.

OUR COOK DAYA

I remember Daya our cook well. She would come hurrying into the yard, her soft wrinkling face covered not with the cool morning dew but with the warm sweat of exertion and stress. Her short legs did their best but they had to carry a plump body and as she hurried into our yard her anxiety went ahead of her. On mornings, if she was late, she would hurry in like a strong wind and with a whirling movement exchange her outdoor slippers for her indoor ones, tie on her apron, wash her hands and begin the tidying up of her domain – the kitchen.

I was not there when Daya came for the job as cook, but it is clear that she agreed to come early so that my mother could open the grocery shop at 7.00 a.m. For if Daya was late, it meant that my mother had to be in two places at once: at the shop where early morning customers were always in a hurry for tea, cigarettes, matches, butter and biscuits, cheese, sugar and coffee; and in the kitchen, serving breakfast to us all, including two clerks (who were given board and lodging as they lived in the country). The constant knocking of impatient customers on the shop counter with their coins infuriated my mother and so Daya, if she was late, received the full pent-up charge of that fury.

Fortunately my mother's anger was like thunder. Rumblings were loud and had to be noted, but when they had passed they were no more. Daya, knowing this, kept her head down and busied herself, saying nothing.

But Daya was not the only one who had to come on time in order that our household might have a smooth start; Baboo the milkman had to be at us by 6.35 a.m. or else he too would be told how he had inconvenienced us all, particularly my father, who breakfasted on fresh milk. He never sat down to breakfast, but had an egg nog, a swizzled mixture of warm milk, one fresh egg, a tablespoon of brandy and a dash of grated nutmeg, which I brought to him from the kitchen to wherever he might be: the bedroom, sitting before a marble table, getting the previous day's takings ready for the bank; or in the shop, making up the accounts of our credit customers, who were many. He took it and drank until the huge cup was drained and the froth escaped to his upper lip.

By seven in the morning, if Daya was on time, our household was like a healthy beehive. But there were days when Daya was very late and the morning was marred by my mother's quarrelling, followed by an uneasy sad silence.

One morning, in the midst of such a silence, I sat down with Daya while she removed the entrails of a young chicken.

'You know, Kam,' she said, 'I got up since five o'clock with the alarm. Didi doesn't know that.' Although I didn't say anything she must have read my thoughts.

'I have to knead the flour and make six good-size roti. And when I finish that, I have to make a big pot of *baigan* and *aloo* and saltfish.'

'He does eat a lot,' I said.

'Yes Kam. He does have to work real hard. Task work in the cane field is hard you know.'

35

'He does eat six roti one time?'

'He does eat two for breakfast and does carry two for lunch. And in the evening when he comes home, I does still be here and he does be hungry.'

I felt sorry for her and told my mother how much work Daya had to complete before she came to us. My mother said nothing. The next time Daya came a little late she also said nothing.

Another day when Daya was kneading flour, she gave me some dough and while I was busy with it, remembering my Plasticine days, she said: 'I want you to do something for me, Kam.'

I was engrossed with the dough and so nodded my willingness. It was the way she whispered the request that I knew it was going to be work for a conspirator.

'On Friday I want you to go to the rum shop and see if he there.

'And what to do when I see him?'

'You come back straight here and tell me.'

'All you vex?'

'Kam, that man go be the death of me. You know how hard I does work to keep him looking good? Everybody telling him how good he looking since he take up with me. I does wash for him, clean, everything, everything I tell you, Kam. Only me know.'

I nodded in full agreement and gave her full and heavy sighs of my support.

'You do too much for him,' I said, busying myself with cutting up the dough in thin long pieces.

'I does do more than too much.'

'You too good to him. You treat him too good and he doesn't appreciate it.' *Appreciate* was a word often used in my village. I grew up to feel that more often than not most people did not appreciate something or other.

'He isn't accustomed to good treatment, Kam.'

I agreed wholeheartedly with two nods of my head.

'You know his family, Kam? They don't care about him, but once they hear he going with me, they coming round the house pretending to care for him. You know when I start to go with him – and this is only between the two of us – now don't tell anyone, you hear me – he didn't have anything at all, nothing he could put his hands on, and say, "Well, this is mine." It was I, Kam, I, who saved and scraped and saved and scraped and if you see the house now, you wouldn't believe it is the same house. You haven't seen the house?'

I shook my head knowing that she meant, not the outside of the house which I knew, but inside her home.

'One of these days you must come.'

Friday came and as midday approached it was clear that Daya did not have her mind on her work. She had made an arrangement with her husband, as she called him, to call at the gate and bring her his week's wage. As midday came and went she asked me to go to my father's rum shop and see if he was there.

I didn't like doing it but as Daya had explained:

'He expects meat and fish and, you know, last week, he asking for salad – salad mind you. How to do that, that's my problem when he drinks all the money, Kam.'

I think I know a little of how Judas must have felt when I crossed the railway line and passed the school. In 1940, my father had built a brand new rum shop at the corner of Eastern Main Road and Pasea Road and this was where I was going. It had smelt so good and right then; new timber and fresh paint; everything clean and bright. There were special store rooms for the barrels of rum and the boxes of clean empty bottles and labels. There were private rooms with tables and jalousied bar doors. I was two and a half when it was built and had difficulty stretching my legs to climb the high concrete step. There were two outdoor lavatories in the large back yard, and even here was freshness and cleanliness and newness; though this was not to last long. As my mother said, 'The public is too undisciplined.'

Daya's husband, when sober, was the gentlest of men, shy with the smile of a boy of six and quite innocent of conspiracies. So it was with mixed feelings that I arrived at the rum shop. The first gush of warm intoxication overpowered me and I felt uncomfortable and dizzy. It was as if an entire cask of rum had recently been spilt and been absorbed by its walls, the men, the air and the wooden floor. Although I was only seven at the time, and unaware of much in the adult world, I felt, the minute I entered the shop, that I ought to leave at once, and would have done so but for Daya.

There were men at the wide wooden counter, sitting in groups of twos and threes. There were small tables forming a wider circumference around the counter and these too were all filled. I did not see Daya's husband. But I knew there were several private rooms inside, which I couldn't possibly enter and where he might be. There were two ladies, brightly dressed, like flamboyant birds, sitting with a circle of men. Everyone was talking together. The air was noisy and warm, a fusion of rum and men, smoke, song and oysters, pepper sauce, *chatni*, *bara* and *pholourie*.

'What you want?' asked the clerk David.

'Is Daya husband here?'

'She send you?'

'She wants some money to buy goods,' I heard myself say. 'She doesn't have anything in the house and she doesn't like trust.' I was astonished at how easily words come to conspirators.

'Well, he inside with a few friends. But don't say I tell you, eh.'

I nodded and ran off with this precious information. As soon as I opened the gate I cried out, 'Daya, he there.' She waited for me to enter the kitchen. 'You saw him?'

'Yes.'

'He saw you?'

'No.'

'Thank you, Kam. I am grateful, child. You are a good girl.' I nodded in agreement.

Very quickly she untied her apron, exchanged her indoor slippers for her outdoor ones, looked at her face in the mirror, and moved both her hands over her head as if brushing it. All the while she spoke: 'Kam, I does feel so bad I tell you, a decent lady like me inside a rum shop. But what can I do?'

I remained silent.

'When I get there, what you think I will find? He buying drinks for everybody who come round him. Sometimes he buying for everybody on the counter. And when the money done, you think he seeing them? That man so foolish. You know how much I does talk to him? But is like talking to the wind.' And she moved very fast, her short legs doing their best to take her plump body along. I couldn't help thinking that she looked like our fat duck rushing to gobble up something tasty it had seen.

Daya had good Fridays and bad Fridays. On the good Fridays, her husband came to the gate, called out to her and brought her his wage. She, in return, handed him enough for three drinks. He would then walk away slowly after unsuccessfully asking for more. Her bad Fridays were when she had to hurry to the rum shop before he spent it all. Because her bad days brought her so much misery I once said to her:

'Daya, you should leave your husband. He is no good.' She did not say anything and being only seven I did not understand the meaning of the silence, so I continued: 'He will be the death of you,' using her oft repeated phrase.

'How I go leave him, Kam? He doesn't have anybody to look after him.' I had not thought of that but I was adamant.

'Let his family who coming round, coming round, look after him.'

'Them, Kam? They like soucouyant. They go suck him dry. People like them...' and she shook her head sadly, 'they no good, Kam. Take it from me.'

From that day on Daya went up in my estimation. I felt here was a woman struggling so hard to build a home and a relationship with someone not appreciative of her. But she held on and, orphan as she was, appreciated more than I could ever have understood then, the importance of having at least one human being, however imperfect, as a close companion.

'Kamla,' my mother says, 'it is time.' My eyes, heavy with sleep, do not stir, yet I know what I must do. My younger brothers and sister sleep on.

The cold morning air and the electric bulb of the open gallery face me. From behind her long silky black hair I hear my mother say, 'The soap, I left it.' Already showered, armed with a rolled up towel, and head bent, she is beating out the water from her hanging hair.

'There is a towel too,' she adds. Wrapped in my housecoat I go outside. The electric bulb from the gallery does not penetrate far into the night; it does not reach the outdoor bathroom. I open its galvanized sheet door and look up. There are only a few stars left looking in at me. I wink and from that distance they respond. 'Hurry up,' my mother calls. I jump and turn the tap on. The enormous shower head, the size of the moon, frets and fumes, angry at being awakened yet again at four in the morning. The cold water rushes out. I hesitate and with all the determination of a seven year old enter the arena of needle-cold sprays.

Out I come like a drenched hen, sneezing and trembling. My mother is busy moving about from the kitchen to the shop. 'When you are finished, pick the flowers and remember what I told you.'

The day before I had decided what I was going to wear. I knew it had to be clean and simple and preferably white. Dressed and carrying a wooden tray I go out to pick the flowers. In the darkness I am afraid of stepping on a frog or having one plop on me. So, seeing nothing, I make low, threatening, primeval noises, hoping that any nearby frogs will hop away in the opposite direction. But fearing that this may not be enough, I stamp the earth, wishing my feet had the authority of an elephant's.

I stand in the dark, before the tall ixora shrub and gently shake a branch and whisper: 'Ma is going to the *siwala*. I have come for some flowers.' My mother had said that I should first gently awaken the tree and ask its permission, not rouse it rudely by pulling flowers from its sleeping branches. I pause, awaiting a reply. The cool morning breeze shakes the leaves and a slender branch bows. I fill the tray with large red balls of ixoras.

Two gleaming brass *lotas,* one large and the other small, have been prepared for offering by my mother, with rice, flowers, leaves, a silver coin, *supari* and other things. 'Don't fill them with water yet,' she says.

We close the crooked gate behind us and turn right, onto the gravelly earth road to the temple. We meet no one on our way. The houses look like shadows and the railway line sleeps. A stray dog comes up to us, sniffs and runs off. Far far away a cock crows. It is cool and the air is fresh and strong and passes over me like a deep wave some distance from the shore.

'You must empty your mind of everyday things and concentrate on God,' my mother says.

'Yes,' I reply, for I am feeling good, refreshed and devout with my hands completely encircling the now warm *lota* of flowers. We climb the embankment and cross the railway line, the rails beaded with dew drops. We can see the brightly glowing temple, partly hidden by taller buildings, is keeping the surrounding darkness at bay.

As we approach the main road we see a neat row of beggars sitting silently on the pavement. Yet, as in a market place, a growing buzz of activity is everywhere. There are stalls of planks and boxes and tarpaulin, lit by hanging lanterns, flambeaux, wall lamps and pitch-oil lamps. The aroma of sweet bubbling syrup and intoxicating garlands of marigolds and temple flowers warms the air and I feel very comfortable. There are many tents with Indian sweetmeats: *pehra, gulabjamun, jilebi* and my favourite, *ladhu,* all neatly arranged. Blocks of *pehra* are displayed like an Egyptian pyramid. There are savouries too: *bara, pholourie, kachowrie,* all served with a mouth-watering tamarind and mango *chatni.*

I begin to feel hungry as I see and hear the swish and sizzle of the boiling oil which transforms everything into crispy delights. Three vendors hail out, entreating us to taste their wares. My mother with one waft of her hand dismisses them all.

We arrive at Rama's large stall. I know Ma buys all her household sweets from him and whenever she is having something special at home like a *katha,* puts through a large order. Rama is thin and immaculately dressed. His white apron glistens with brushes of white sugar crystals; so too do those of his two young sons. The boys smile when they see my mother approaching. Their smiles still linger when they look at me.

Rama gets up from a chair at the back of his tent, he looks very tired but still comes to the counter and greets my mother, saying in Hindi, 'What will you have today, Maharajin?'

'Just give me three of everything.' He knows that by everything she means the usual ones she buys. As he carefully places them in a two pound brown paper bag he says again in Hindi, 'Is that all you will have today?'

'This is for the *siwala;* afterwards we will come back.'

'Very well.'

He turns his attention to me and speaks in English. 'So you come too to celebrate *Shivaratri,* the birth of Lord Shiva?'

I nod.

'It is a good thing, Maharajin, to bring the children. You have to introduce the young to their own tradition.' He pauses and weighs the sweets.

'You have to start young,' he says again, 'for by the time they reach fourteen-fifteen it is already too late.'

My mother makes a movement of the head which says these are well established ideas and I do not disagree with you. She offers to pay him but he says, 'When you come back.'

He turns to me. 'You must pray for me.' I stand and stare. 'Will you pray for me?' he asks again. His two young sons, not much older than I, are looking at me and smiling shyly. Everyone is now looking at me. I clasp my small *lota* more tightly not knowing what is expected of me. He has asked me nicely, I say to myself, and he sells such delicious sweets. I look at him and nod. 'Good girl,' he says and claps his hands. We leave the stall; I walking behind my mother.

As we approach the temple she hands me a long neat tube of tightly parcelled copper coins. We go through the narrow door of the forecourt and there before us are the beggars, closely packed, rows and rows of them. But there is a path, a narrow opening, leading to the inner temple. We fill our *lotas* with water from the tap in the forecourt.

The beggars sit 'yoga-style' or squat on jute bags, once filled with sugar or rice. White flour bags with 'Canada' printed in red block letters are also spread out. In front of each beggar, on a piece of white cotton cloth, there is a low mound of rice, perhaps about one and a half pounds; those who give alms drop the coins on the rice where they are held fast and do not roll away.

The bright lights, the dazzling white cotton, and the large number of people all round trouble me; I'm not quite sure what to do. I hear myself saying, 'Let us give to those at the back row; these here in the front get all the time.'

'How to get there, that is the problem.'

'We'll have to push through.'

My mother looks at the difficulty of negotiating a way through the mass of people and is angry.

'Who told them to sit so far? They can't see nobody can get there?'

'They have nowhere else to sit.'

One of the beggars in the front row says to her, 'Where you going? There is no place to pass.'

My mother says, 'It is no use.' I stand there feeling uncomfortable and unhappy. 'Shift a little. I am going through,' I hear my mother say. I am awakened and excited. The man moves his shoulder only; my mother becomes cross. 'Look here,' she says loudly, addressing everyone, 'give me a little chance, I want to get to the back.' I follow. She decides to make it worthwhile for those who enable her to pass through. All around people are stretching out their thin swaying hands, like long grass in the wind.

We move with great difficulty. Several times I feel it is a bad idea. After much stretching over and almost losing her balance twice, my mother reaches the back. One of the men thanks God, another is asleep, many are in a quiet daze as if looking at a film invisible to us.

It is not easy getting out either. When we finally do, my mother says, 'I am not going back there again, you can go if you want.'

'Those in the front get everything,' I reply.

'Whose fault is that?'

I have no coins left and with my mother join the queue to the inner temple.

'Here,' she says, handing me a smaller roll of tightly compressed silver coins.

In the gallery, before the inner sanctum, a pile of slippers and chappals stands. 'Take your slippers off,' I hear my mother say, but these are new slippers and truly beautiful, from China or was it Japan? I had hoped to be able to hide them somewhere.

'Nobody will take your slippers, beti,' says a lady behind me. 'You are now in the House of God, no one will do that.'

'Yes,' says another, whose slippers would tempt no one. 'Look at me, I am not afraid.'

'She is only a child,' a voice says. I remove my slippers and put them next to the wall. I lift two slippers and place them one on top of the other, so completely covering mine.

As I stand before the narrow door the scent of incense, burnt ghee and the fragrance of a thousand gardens wafts through I can see from over my mother's shoulders that the gods are overladen with flowers.

It is now my mother's turn. She steps forward, hands the parcel of sweets to a *sadhu* in the corner. He blesses her and puts a *tika* on her forehead. She returns and faces the god Shiva. He stands before her, in the form of an enormous elongated sphere of warm-coloured crystalline metamorphic rock. She bows her head and closes her eyes.

I look around the temple and see that the gods and their spouses are standing in a circle. Earlier, when I got up in the darkness, I had thought that I was going to be amongst the devout few, but now, when I look around and see so many offerings, flowers everywhere, overflowing from the altars and ledges on to the floor, I am a little taken aback that so many were here before me.

As I stand behind my mother, she seems so lonely and vulnerable. I think I know what she is saying to Shiva. My father has diabetes and my brother is away at Grant Medical College in Bombay and she wants him to help them both. I wonder what else she is saying. She thinks of so many people in her prayers. I turn around with a nervous smile, trying to observe if there are impatient devotees. I decide that if she is long I will be quick.

She ends her prayers and pours her offerings on Shiva's head, looks up, and rings the overhanging bell. It resounds powerfully within the enclosed space. I wonder whether this is meant to awaken the gods lest they fall asleep from sheer exhaustion on such auspicious days. I decide that I too will ring the bell.

My mother turns to the right to make her offerings to the other gods. It is now my turn:

I too bow my head and close my eyes and say, 'Dear God, please do not let me fall ill. Help my mother and father and my brother. Make them wise and good and healthy and me too. Give me much understanding. When I marry let me marry someone kind and good and let me also be kind and good. And please help me to learn my spelling well.' I can think of nothing else to say and I begin to think that perhaps I have already been too long. I pour my offerings and give the bell a good push. The sound is embarrassingly loud. I try to move quickly away, but there is nowhere to hide and I must take my turn in the queue to Bramha. I am too close to the bell. The *sadhu,* half asleep in the corner, jumps and looks at me angrily, shaking his head and forefinger in disapproval. I believe Shiva will be more understanding.

It was only when I was a yard from Rama's sweet counter that I realised I had not prayed for him. I felt terrible. 'What will I say if he asks?' I could not face him with this truth. I had to think quickly. What could I say? I decided to say that I had, and that when I got home I would make proper amends. His two sons were smiling sweetly.

'Crowded, isn't it?' the older boy said. He had already acquired the skill of easy communication with customers.

'Where is your father?' my mother asked.

'He had to go home.'

'He is sick,' the younger son added.

'Your father works too hard,' my mother said sadly.

I felt worse. How would God respond to my plan?

'We know. He has always worked hard. That's his way,' the elder replied. The younger joined in. 'The doctor says he should rest. But he does not know how to rest.' There was an awkward silence. What could we say to these diligent sons on behalf of this worthy, ailing man who had worked all his life making excellent sweets and who could not stop because he had a family to keep up. 'Well, what will you have?' the older son asked.

On our way home, people were opening their windows and filling oil tins and buckets with water at the standpipe. I wanted to say to some I knew, that I had been to the temple, but there was no way of saying this except to swing my *lota* about, which I did. No one noticed except my mother. 'Kamla stop that.'

When we reached home I sat in the hammock and, with my mouth full of *ladhu,* started to swing. My mother went to the back garden and fed the ants sweet yellow crystals of Demerara sugar. Later I remembered Rama before the sacred Tulsi tree.

PART TWO

AND DARKNESS FALLS

SILENCE IS GOLDEN

I am not sure how it happened, it must have been a gradual thing, but over the years school became as sombre and as sad a place as an open prison. The moment I entered the school yard, I was in another world with its own beliefs, rules and aspirations boldly stated in chalk on every wall:

Manners maketh man. Eat meat, milk, eggs and cheese daily. Money is the root of all evil. A penny saved is a penny gained. Speak quietly for quiet speech is a sign of refinement. Always respect your elders. Neither a lender nor a borrower be. Drink six glasses of fresh water daily. Everything comes to him who sits and waits. Reach for the stars.

And there were the proverbs on my classroom wall:

Honesty is the best policy. To thine own self be true. Perseverance wins. The devil finds work for idle hands to do, and many many more, enough to fill up my exercise book.

Just in case there were pupils who had eyes but saw not, we were given essays to write on these proverbs, and during morning assembly stories were told which encouraged self-sacrifice and hard work. To those who could not measure up to these requirements corporal punishment awaited, in this world and the next.

A typical morning assembly story went like this – 'Once two boys applied to a store for a job; they were interviewed by the manager who did not know which one to choose as they were both nice lads, neatly dressed and behaving with proper courtesy. On their way out they noticed that a number of items had fallen from a shelf. One of the boys felt that was not his business, but the other made it his business, he stayed behind and replaced them neatly on the shelf.'

No one needed to be told who got the job, but the reasons for the manager's choice were further expounded to us.

It was not long before I found myself in Standard Two. Our teacher, Miss Mills, was high coloured and very pleased with her red African hair; she was always touching it and looking at it in a small mirror. She was also the school's music teacher and carried a tuning fork in her handbag to prove it.

Miss Mills taught us the French and the American national anthems. The British national anthem we knew well, for we were British. The government said so.

We were also taught seventeenth century English songs: 'Cherry ripe cherry ripe, ripe, I cry, full and fair ones come and buy'; and 'Where the bee sucks there suck I'. There were other beautiful songs: 'Who is Sylvia, What is she?', 'The Ashgrove How Gentle'. Christmas carols; and nursery rhymes like 'Who killed Cock Robin?' and 'Do you ken John Peel?' which made no sense to me, and hundreds more.

We also learnt deeply moving Negro spirituals and sad, soulful songs from the Black American South: 'Carry me back to Old Virginy', 'Swing Low Sweet Chariot', 'The Sun Shone Bright on my old Kentucky Home', 'Nobody Knows the Trouble I seen', 'Old Man River' and many many more. We were filled with music, even the popular songs like, 'I'm going to take you on a slow boat to China', and 'Beautiful Dreamer'. But there were no songs from India.

Despite the dust, heat and humidity, everything about Miss Mills was clean. She changed her frocks daily and wore petticoats of white satin, lace and ribbons. This she showed us when she cleaned her glasses: first removing them, then lifting a small circumference of her skirt's hem, and finally by using a portion of the revealed undergarment to polish them. She would lift these glasses up to the sunlight and with half-closed eyes examine the progress made.

A number of boys in Miss Mills' class were far too big for the desks. Their difficulty lay in their legs and thighs. They preferred to sit at the back. From time to time they would lose their rubbers, money, or pencils and would spend ages under the desk searching for fallen items. One would eventually rise up from the floor like a successful pearl diver, others would giggle, change colour and behave strangely until Miss Mills, noticing the commotion, would walk around to see how far we had reached in the exercise set.

It was a time for learning by rote, not only poetry and spelling, conversion tables of pounds and dollars, definitions of parts of speech, proverbs and similes, but everything else. A good memory was all one needed to escape caning. Young Ramswammy from our village observed this and began to learn the words and meanings of our entire school dictionary. He told me this when he had reached the letter J.

'Why?' I asked him.

He looked at me and smiled kindly at the naivety of my question.

'It is only a matter of time,' he said and, seeing I was not impressed, added, 'When the day comes and we are asked to start with the dictionary, remember I forecast it; me, Ramswammy.' And he pointed to his narrow chest. 'Besides, I would not be in trouble then,' and he smiled, observing my discomfort.

There is no doubt we attained a very high standard in arithmetic but we did it by working mechanically and without thinking; for each type of problem there were over a hundred examples to do. So we arrived at an answer in much the same way as we arrived at a friend's house. We had no understanding of the principles which underlay our results, which we could always check by referring to the answers at the back of the text.

It was a time when reasons for things were not given. It was a time when everyone politely accepted what was said. We were reaping the harvest of the time before. Teachers them-selves, when young, had not been given any reasons for things, and later found that they too, like their teachers before them, could manage in the classroom without asking 'why?'

And so throughout our school life we were given ideas, concepts, values, formulae. We received them and were later told that we had received an education. Because of this, we could neither assess nor give meaning to things: even our own history or that of the misnomer, the 'New World', the Americas so close to us. We did not understand why things were as they were. To us the British Empire and the sun had certain common features and we accepted them both as the natural order. My father lined up at school to welcome the Prince of Wales, Prince Edward, and I did the same for Princess Margaret Rose.

As I grew taller I began to think there was something contrary in the way my mind worked. It began innocently at first (or so I thought) to question quite simple things. For example, I felt that in the proverb, 'An early bird catches the worm', one had to decide whether one was a bird or a worm, and if a worm, one should be on the look out for early birds.

And then this contrary mind would ask, 'For a worm, what should the proverb be?' I could see that the proverb looked at the world from the stance of the bird, the fleet of foot and the strong of beak; but this very annoying voice within me would ask the same question again. 'Think. Were you a worm, a lowly blind living thing, what would your saying be?' And to my surprise the voice in me said, 'A wise worm will hide when the birds do glide.'

The presence of such an inner voice is not the sort of thing you would wish to speak about, and I had no way of knowing whether anyone I knew had one. So, unwillingly, I carried mine in silence.

There were times I wished I could very gently remove it from me and place it on a tree. I reasoned that were I to place it there, I could ask it questions when I wanted to, concerning things that were safe to talk about. But to always carry one's inner voice about is a heavy burden and one I did not want.

To add to my anxiety I had seen in a film called Joan *Of Arc* what happened to a young woman who admitted publicly that she had listened to her inner voice. And my mother, whenever something tragic occurred in the neighbourhood, would say, 'Kamla, you should learn from the experiences of others,' and added, 'Only fools do not.'

This contrary voice came up again during a West Indian

history lesson. I was in Standard Four. The class was at ease and Mr. Braithwaite, our teacher, had talked about the English explorer, Sir Walter Raleigh, and the privateer, Sir Francis Drake, and we were now on Sir John Hawkins and the slave trade.

In front of us were drawings of the cross section of a slave ship, from which we saw how tightly the slaves were packed. When I learned they were chained together my inner voice began asking, 'What happened when one of them wished to go to the lavatory?' It was not a pleasant question, so I ignored it. But before I could stop it, I heard my inner voice say quite clearly to Mr. Braithwaite: 'Sir, why should the Queen of England honour with a knighthood men like Sir John Hawkins who started the slave trade to the West Indies and America?'

Mr. Braithwaite lowered his book, removed his glasses, took a crumpled handkerchief from his pocket and said in a learned, slow way, as if the wisdom of his utterance was too weighty to carry, 'The slave trade made England rich and her colonies too.' 'Thank you Sir,' I said and was about to sit down, but evidently my inner voice was not satisfied either with this answer or with me for I heard it say:

'Excuse me, Sir, doesn't it matter how a nation gets rich?' and while Mr. Braithwaite, who in his past life must have been a snail, was engaged yet again in removing his glasses; before he spoke, my inner voice said, 'The really important thing is to become rich and powerful; is that what England is saying?'

Anyone who knew Mr. Braithwaite could see that he had a secret desire to be a proper English gentleman. It was his clothes and his umbrella and the way he stood up and the way he walked and spoke of Shakespeare and Wordsworth and daffodils, even as he stared at red dancing hibiscus in the school yard. Later I understood this human feeling, this preference to be amongst the higher ups, but when he said:

'Insolent girl! Insolent! You will write one hundred times, "I must respect my betters"; that will teach you to keep a civil tongue in that foolish head of yours,' I was stunned. I felt he had struck me. My pencil fell and I bent and tried to soothe my

53

bruised spirit; but no longer was I able to follow the rest of the lesson; a misty film had come between me and the tightly packed slave ship.

Because of this experience, and not wishing my inner voice to surprise me again, I devised a simple method to silence it: singing a merry tune loudly. At first my inner voice struggled with the quick tempo of my chosen tunes, but with intense concentration and by increasing the strength of my public voice I was able to smother it. But it simply bided its time and came upon me as a gentle friend at night; and when I sat alone on the edge of the quiet brook, hidden by tall grass, looking at the darting fishes, or when I sat high up in a mango tree, camouflaged by leaves and branches, it whispered things to me, difficult things I could not answer: 'If I were a bird and flew on and on past the blues of the sky, what would I find? What are the stars made of? Could someone drill a hole so deep that the drill would appear exposed on the other side of the earth? Does God really know what everyone is thinking everywhere, from the tundra to the Himalayas to the Pygmies? Who made God? Where did he come from? Who were his parents?'

Throughout the 1940s and 1950s hundreds of Red Indian and Cowboy films were shown on Trinidadian film screens. At play, at school and at home, everyone wanted to be Cowboys, for we all knew how the games must end. It was not easy to get anyone to play Red Indians. I wanted the Red Indians to win because, with the help of a history book called *People from Far-off Lands,* I had learnt to see them as simple nomadic peoples. In these films I could see that Red Indians were losing their land to invaders who thought nothing of lying and cheating and killing for their own ends and who wished to grab the Continent and all that was in it.

And there was another ugly thing. These 'Westerns' portrayed Red Indians as savages and not what they really were: simple nomadic peoples fighting for their very survival; for their land, their way of life; for their sons and daughters against hordes of brutish robbers.

One film in particular, where large numbers of Red Indians were brutally murdered because they trusted the word of a wily trader, greatly distressed me. I returned home about eight at night and sat down in the hammock. There I quietly wept for Red Indians who had been cruelly slaughtered over a hundred years ago. I wept that no one cared. I wept that they should be portrayed as savages. My mother sat with me; she thought I was ill, and coaxed me gently to have some milk for I had lost the desire to eat. The sheer continental size of their loss struck my mind a staggering blow.

I tried to make sense of these atrocities but was unable to do so. I could not understand how we could accept such things. I could not understand how a people could lose everything they had, even their lives, and be called savages in their attempt to defend their family, their land and themselves. But I least understood how men could be so barbaric, so iniquitous, that after unjustly decimating millions they could see themselves as just, upright and fair. And yet all these things had come to pass and all these ugly things were given a nonsense name: 'The discovery of the New World'.

As the stars looked in at me, I asked: 'Why didn't you do something to assist?' I heard the flap-flapping of our *jhandi* and turned to the god Shiva: 'Why? Why millions? Please explain.' The night was cold and soft and the *jhandi* continued to make its presence heard. But I received neither comfort nor understanding.

For a very long time after, I was terrified of Americans; I saw them as savages. When in the 1940s American soldiers stationed in Trinidad threw packages of chewing gum and silver and copper coins out of train windows to us children on the railway embankment, I was suspicious, and would not be taken in by those smiling gum-chewing men. Standing on the embankment, alone, I watched these passing trains and would not scramble for such deserts. Barefoot, with the wind in my hair, I made my stand for a people who were no more.

55

Mr. Skinner, the Deputy Headmaster, had the energy of a demon. He would think nothing of lining up the entire senior school, four hundred children, and administering two lashes each with a heavy black leather strap. He did not leave this to chance, he engineered situations for which, in the 1940s, the administration of corporal punishment was considered reasonable. I used to think that one day he would be tired, very tired, and would have to say to the next in line, 'You are lucky; I am tired.'

That unfortunately never happened.

As term came to an end he would bring the whole school together, and call out:

'Would someone from Standard One come up here on the platform and either recite a poem or sing a song. I will count up to ten.' If no one came up by the time Mr. Skinner reached ten, the entire class marched on to the platform where he stood, and received two lashes each.

There were some children for whom the fear of appearing on a platform before the entire school was shattering. But there were those who feared corporal punishment even more. Children with the latter fear would come to the platform by the count of eight. They might have been hoping that someone in the class would be braver than they; but seeing the possibility of that fading, would decide to enter the arena and face the bull.

On one occasion I was very surprised to see my cousin Satrohan walking up the platform at the count of seven. He looked like someone walking to the guillotine, propelled forward by unseen currents, as in a dream. Anyone who knew Satrohan would have been taken aback that this over-shy, gentle boy had dared to think of walking onto the platform. Even in the comfort and security of his own home, he had very little to say. He had a stammer which under stress grew into something unkind.

As Satrohan climbed the movable stairs, they shook, but he

walked without hesitation; at eight, he had become a man with a mission.

'When I was sick and lay in bed, I had two pillows at my head.' So he began.

Now the standard of recitation in our school was high. We all knew the rules: first you bow, then pause, then give the title of the poem clearly for all to hear and this must be followed by the poet's name. After this, a slight pause before beginning.

But Satrohan did none of these things and to increase his problems further, at the end of the first stanza, nothing followed. He simply bowed and walked off the stage. Fear of being beaten had forced him on to the platform and now fear had locked his memory. This one stanza was his offering. It was all he had. Inside me something began to tighten and hurt. I knew he could not withstand that heavy leather strap coming down upon him with the force of Mr. Skinner's muscular right arm. Not all boys could. Some screamed out openly, others dashed out of school and one brave lad attempted to defend himself with his fist – but paid too dearly before a packed assembly hall for his spirit's spontaneous rebellion.

We awaited Mr. Skinner's recall of Satrohan. We knew the outcome of such a lapse. Three seconds passed; and then it was that old, bespectacled Mrs. Rattan arose. She did not enjoy good health but she was Satrohan's class teacher. There she stood as lithe as a bamboo awaiting a storm. She clapped and nodded to her class to do the same. As if on cue everyone joined in; the thunderous clamour rushed down like an avalanche onto the platform threatening to cover Mr. Skinner, but he stood unmoved.

We all waited. We knew he could do anything if he felt his authority was being defied. He glared at Mrs. Rattan; she looked back, but not with defiance. She looked at him with gentleness, in her eyes a liquid trust like that a trapped fawn might show to her hunter. She smiled only with her eyes and nodded so softly to him it seemed like an unseen caress. He fingered the knot of his tie and stared at the clock. He ascended the rostrum and faced the school: 'Next. Standard Two,' he roared, 'and this time no short cuts.' Without warning, he bent his head and chuckled with his shoulders and stomach and we smiled to help him to chuckle more. Mrs. Rattan with her beaming brimming eyes applauded him. Satrohan lifted his head. I wondered whether Mrs. Rattan should have been a lion tamer. She made us girls feel that even old ladies who are at times wobbly on their feet had much to offer.

I used to think, as I have said, that Mr Skinner would one day give up flogging pupils because of sheer exhaustion but that was before I observed him closely and saw how much he enjoyed the feel of the strap. It was the way he ran his left hand over it again and again, as if approving its qualities of length, texture and strength.

There were times after lunch, for example, when his eyes looked a pained red. He might have had a little rum, to stimulate the appetite or to get rid of a cold – excuses grown-ups used when they found themselves drinking before children. Unfortunately for me Mr. Skinner was not only the Deputy Headmaster; when I got into the Fifth Standard, he became my class teacher. School was transformed. It became a place of mental and physical torture, especially during spelling periods for me, and during arithmetic classes for many others.

Mental arithmetic in particular was a traumatic experience for the class. There could be twelve or twenty arithmetical problems to be solved without the use of pen and paper; it all depended on how Mr. Skinner was feeling that day.

'Pens and pencils down. Sit up,' was the first command. The problem was given: There are two taps: one is filling a tank, the other is emptying it. How long would it take to fill the tank. The length, width and height of the tank were given together with the rate of flows of each tap.

Other favourites of Mr. Skinner were train sums. There are two trains moving in opposite directions. How long would it take (a) both trains to meet and (b) to pass each other. The speed of each train, their lengths as well as their distance apart were stated. You were allowed to pick up your pen only to

58

write down the answer. After what seemed like eternity if you were confused, the command came. 'Pens and pencils down.' Some people lost concentration and some were really not up to it. They could work it out on paper but not mentally. If you got less than half the sums right you were given two strokes. We did the marking ourselves on an exchange basis.

Of course you could make an arrangement with your neighbour that, were you on the borderline, she would alter one of your answers and you would do the same for her. Because of this, Mr. Skinner preferred us to use a pen and not a pencil. He also changed around those who marked our books. Under his direction, it was a different marker each time. We would have to give our books to those at the front, at the back, the sides or to those in completely different rows. We had no way of telling who our marker would be. But what messages mere trifles conveyed – a nod, a smile, a wink; we were conspirators and had no need for words.

Despite Mr. Skinner's fine cunning, some of us developed finer skills of turning a 'five' into an 'eight' or a 'one' into virtually any number. Knowing which numbers to avoid when in doubt was helpful. But despite much ingenuity on our part, many of us had to face the hard wrinkled leather strap.

Although I was good at mental arithmetic and at reciting poems before the school, spelling was my Achilles heel. I had a great fear of being beaten and Mr. Skinner's long strap was for me an instrument of terror. I hated it. I had witnessed particularly brutal forms of corporal punishment administered by teachers and parents, which had left children quivering and whimpering. This execution of the human spirit affected me greatly.

Understandably I took pains to learn my spelling but the mere presence of Mr. Skinner was enough to create doubt and hesitancy as to the spelling of a word about which I had been certain in the cool quiet walks of our vegetable garden. Oral spelling tests were held on Thursdays at 2 p.m. At that time of the day, the sun is fierce and angry and smoke rises from the pitched asphalt roads; distant glare dazzles. It is a time when birds and dogs sleep soundly, not opening even one eye when you stand before them.

But we in Standard Five would be wide awake, jumping and bouncing as drops of water on a red hot plate. On this particular Thursday, for some reason we were especially anxious as we waited outside in the dusty school yard for Mr. Skinner to take his class. Three girls could not contain their anxieties. They jumped up and down as if possessed and were tiring to look at. Two others made a dash to the lavatory. The entire class was buzzing with sounds of letters of the alphabet. Thirty-five ten year olds stood under a spreading mahogany tree, grouped in a semicircle broken in places by the anxious movements of the wretched.

No one appeared to be looking directly at the open corridor which led from the school to the yard, yet the moment Mr. Skinner hurried into it, the entire class knew. Words were hurled into our semicircle like stones, 'He's coming.' Then, 'Oh my God!' followed by a wild scramble. Quickly pages would be turned. A last look at a difficult word, then another and another. Some wrote a code letter with their toes on the ground, of no significance to anyone but themselves.

Whether he sensed our fear I cannot tell, for his voice was measured and calm. He pulled his curled smooth hard strap from his pocket and flexed it in preparation for the task ahead. Then the dreaded command came: 'Close books.' As if shuffling a pack of cards he held the leather strap in both hands, furling and unfurling it. 'If you have tears prepare to shed them now,' he said. A lost bird flew past, calling. In the stillness of the afternoon heat he tested the strap several times – vwhop-vwhop – into the air. I didn't know those much repeated words were Shakespeare's. I thought, we all thought then, that they were Mr. Skinner's.

There were twenty-five words all told, but standing before Mr. Skinner, each correct letter making up a word became a single step to salvation. But letters were also traps laid to confuse and ensnare. Words with a silent *p* as in *psalm* and *pneumonia;* words with no relationship to sound as in *lieuten-*

ant; barbaric sounding syllables of *eath* and *eigh* as in *beneath* and *neigh.* Why couldn't it have been *nay? Ough* was another such discomforting sound as in *thorough.* Then there were words which do not need to be spelt, where one letter from the alphabet would have sufficed as in *queue.* And there was the overpowering difficulty *of diarrhoea.*

As we did not know from which end of the semicircle Mr. Skinner would begin, there was usually a fight for the middle ground by the bullies and the crafty. Jacob a tall tough-looking but gentle lad stood next to me. 'Jacob,' Mr. Skinner shouted, 'When you grow up, would you like to be a sergeant or a lieutenant?' Jacob, was not a stupid boy, but Mr. Skinner's methods diminished him like a scythe swinging into wholesome stalks of grain.

Jacob's school day was usually a long embarrassment and some teachers enjoyed humiliating him. He grinned and waited to be told which word Mr. Skinner wished him to spell. They were both in the arena. One was equipped for the slaughter, the other did not even have a shield. This was the rule of the game. Mr. Skinner said, 'Don't you know what you want to do when you grow up?' Jacob shook his head. 'A big boy like you should, Jacob.' There was a substantial pause. 'Alright let us ask the class what they think you would be.'

Way way in the distance a donkey began to bray. Someone giggled. Then Jacob spoke, 'A sergeant, please sir.'

'Good. Well spell police sergeant.'

'Police is not on the....'

'That's right. Well spell lieutenant.'

'A sergeant please sir.'

'Yes Jacob I heard you, but I am asking you to spell lieutenant.'

Jacob put his hands out; the sound bounced off his palm vwhop-vwhop. It was now my turn. A part of me had already withered.

'Lieutenant, Kamla.'

'L-i-e-u-t-e-n-a-n-t.'

'Diarrhoea.'

I had made a number of small observations about this word - the two rr's and the hoe aspect at the end – but I could not remember whether there was a letter connecting them.

'Hurry up, I don't have all day. It is not guess work; you either know it or you don't. Come on.' He indicated that I lift my palm. 'Learn your spelling.'

'I learnt it sir.'

'You couldn't have, because if you did, you would know it wouldn't you?'

'I did learn it, sir.'

'Well what is preventing you from saying it?' The half past two train blew its nose and moved on. 'Chocolate water killed meh daughter, chocolate water killed meh daughter,' it sang as it rolled past.

'You are keeping back the whole class.'

I decided to have a go. 'D-i-a-r-r-' and paused. I was left with the sound 'rear' and took a deep breath before, like a nestling, I decided to come out of hiding and make a dash for it; but the hawk was waiting.

'E-h-o-e-a-'

That 'e' was fatal. 'Come on,' he said.

I put out my hand. 'When I say learn your spelling, you must learn your spelling.' 'Vwhop' the strap came down like a vulture's pounce, but my soft moist nine-year-old palm was not there, instead the strap swung through the emptiness of the light warm dusty air and the force of its unimpeded forward strike led to Mr. Skinner tasting the tip – a sip of his own brew.

'If you do that again, you will get two for every one missed.' My palm and wrist blazed; it was the attack and burning sensation of a thousand bacchac ants injecting their poison. My palms began to swell and an inflamed streak was raised. When we were confused we were flogged, when we were frightened we were flogged, and the dull were flogged daily. Tears streamed down my cheeks without my permission and Jacob avoided my face. He bent his head, circling his foot in the dust.

It was during an August school holiday that we went to Whiteland, and it was, as my mother said, 'Way, way, behind God's back.' It may have been its complete isolation (there was only one other household beside the government house) or it may have been the unusual silence of the deep valley, but I felt the experience of this place intensely. I have never seen Whiteland named on a map of Trinidad, but I know it is there and not far removed from a place called Grand Couva, which also does not appear on the maps.

We arrived, a car-load of us, late in the pitch black night: my elder sister, Maya, her husband and two sons, and my younger sister Kavita and I. The moment I opened the car door and rested my feet on loose sand I felt uneasy. We were being watched. The night was still, the eyes silent. Watchful. The journey had been long. Weary and tired, we went straight to bed, but I covered myself with a clean cotton sheet only up to my eyes, for I was now alert. This feeling of being observed by eyes sensed, not seen, stayed with me and I watched the darkness, not through windows – there were none – but through a fine wire mesh. We were caged in.

In the morning I saw it was a place of white sand, yet it was nowhere near the coast. I was thankful that the sun had pierced through the thick encircling forests, but my pleasure went when I discovered that the white sand was infested with jiggers. I had never seen nor heard of such small jumping, hopping parasitic things before and was distressed to learn that they would happily lay their eggs between our toes and on the soles of our feet, or anywhere else. 'They're not fussy,' my sister warned.

There were also giant mosquitoes. The doors and windows of the house were netted to protect us from these carriers of malaria, but, unfortunately, when mosquitoes did get into the house, they were unable to leave – trapped within by the same netting. As they whined, signalling to us that such a space was far too enclosed for them, we had a task which would have challenged a wizard: how to let out those within, and not let in those without. My angry elder sister said, 'This is the kind of house only a government would build. They can't think of little ordinary things, simple common-sense things.'

It was not just the isolation. There was a feeling of threat. Though the house was in a clearing, I could feel the surrounding forest pressing in on us. I felt that we did not belong. One night I dreamt that the forest had quietly crept in upon us and had reached our vulnerable mosquito mesh doors and windows and had begun to push its fine leaves and sticky vines through them. I felt like a fly and the forest a mighty spider with many feelers. It was as if the trees wanted to force us out to make more room for themselves.

I had another unpleasant shock when I discovered that the numerous black fowls which roamed an old disused rubbish dump not far from us were not chickens, as I had thought, but black corbeaux. I had never seen these scavenger birds on the ground before. They had always flown high, well above me; and so, all the time we were there, I felt hemmed in by the corbeaux, the jiggers and the forest.

One Sunday after lunch Maya suggested that all four of us children – her two young sons, Anil and Ashok, and Kavita and I – should go for a walk. I was not too enthusiastic because there was something about the light which made me uneasy. The sun seemed to be playing hide-and-seek behind dark thickening clouds. Suddenly this dark green and light green and yellow green place would become cooler as the midday sun vanished and then reappeared again.

However both my brother-in-law and Maya encouraged us to take a walk and waved us goodbye from their bedroom window, calling out that we should keep to the grassy verge. Waving, we walked past them in single file, because the verge was narrow. As soon as we were out of sight we scampered onto the road which was wide and dry and clean. Occasionally we looked back, just in case my sister decided to follow us for a little while. But she did not come.

So we walked and sang and chatted and shouted and ran

across the road, enjoying the sounds we were making. At first we were careful, checking and rechecking before we made our mad gallop, but it was not long before we felt we were being unduly cautious on a lonely country road.

Soon we became bolder and began to dare one another to lie down on the road which was warm and smooth. We were all lying there enjoying the thrill of danger, when suddenly without warning we heard a loud primeval sound, like a herd of wild elephants rushing towards us.

There was nothing on the road as far as we could see and quickly realised that the sound was coming from the forest. It was then we became aware that the pattern and colour of the clouds had changed drastically. We could see the rain coming towards us in a mantle of mist and billowing black clouds. As the road gave us no protection, we instinctively ran off it, and would have scampered into the forest on our left, but were prevented by a wide ditch between it and the road. We turned to the right and climbed uphill out of the valley. As we climbed, Ashok fell down and began to cry loudly. Frightened and hurt he ran after us. I waited for him.

At last we left the open grassy plains and climbed the higher reaches of the banana plantation where there was some shelter. We jostled together like hens under the broad banana leaves, though we were already soaked by the piercing blasts of fine icy mountain spray. Thunder and wind passed over us, heading towards our home, lashing the thick vegetation until a heavier downpour of rain, sharp and needle-like, fell steadily upon the broad banana leaves. The heavens roared and every shrub swayed and bowed; the wind came and went in bursts; it grew darker and darker. We moved closer together trying to avoid the streams and rivulets funnelled down by leaves, from the higher to the lower like a series of hanging terraces. But if we avoided them we were caught by the full-bodied solitary drops which plop-plopped, either on the ground or on our heads and hands. There was no sky, just streaming water.

It was difficult to know where to stand even after counting the drops, for the wind would change direction and what would appear a good spot would turn out not to be. We were cold and Anil's teeth began to chatter and then his whole body shivered in sympathy. As the eldest, I knew I had to decide whether to stay on and shelter or leave for home through the fury of wind and rain and lightning.

I did not know what to do, and began to feel we had been abandoned, sent out without concern for the signs of the skies. No one said anything. No one coughed. But it was becoming colder and darker and the steady roar of rain continued undiminished. A dense mountain mist veiled the valley and we could not see the road. Lightning struck twice in swift succession.

We waited for the thunder.

Suddenly I remembered old people saying that you shouldn't shelter under a tree because lightning was attracted to them. I had heard of trees that had been split in half or truncated as by a giant swordsman. I realised then that my sister and I were wearing our gold bracelets and gold too, I had been told, attracted lightning. But where does one hide two pairs of gold bracelets? I asked Kavita to remove hers and hand them to me. This she did, her teeth chattering all the while. I unclasped mine and wrapped them all in my wet handkerchief and hid them from view deep in my pocket.

I began to get frightened, wondering whether this downpour was creating dangerous pools and gushing trenches we would not be able to cross. I made up my mind that as soon as the mist lifted we would head for home. This plan I shared with the others and we waited. I could feel that we were intruders and the spirits of the green foliage were the true inhabitants. We did not belong and now we were being punished by the rain, the cold and the wind.

After what seemed like half a day waiting for the mist to lift, I decided on a plan of action. Not without difficulty we pulled and twisted and wrenched off four banana leaves and with each of us holding one above our heads we descended the plateau cautiously, one behind the other, looking like little people of the primeval forest.

There were two large trees at the front of the school building and two enormous spreading ones at the back. Under these trees, but more especially under those at the back, middle-aged ladies would sit with trays of appetising pickled fruit and home-made sweets. Everything on these trays was either one cent or one penny: pickled pomcithre, sweet and sour tamarind, *tolum* and pone, chennet and sugar cake. The sweet and the sour tamarind were both served on pieces of paper cut from a used brown paper bag.

My daily pocket money was one penny. This meant that I could have something from these trays both in the morning and the afternoon recess. Many girls did not have any pocket money, and the toughest amongst them would hang about like spiders waiting to see who would buy these delights. Once you bought, they would surround you jostling and overpowering you. 'Give me a bite,' or 'Give me! Give me.' You had no choice. Often, by the time you had shared it around, you had precious little or nothing left and these spiders, smacking their lips and smiling, moved away from the scene of the kill, pleased with their skill in exacting from others by brute force.

One day I was standing in the school yard and had just peeled off with my teeth a portion of the skin from a box and spice mango. I had taken one bite into that yellow sweetness – sheer nectar, the thick yellow juice spilling over my hands onto my wrist. Suddenly, as from nowhere, I was surrounded by Inez, the gang leader and two other bullies, Monica and Millicent. They surrounded me, pushing their chests closer to me. Inez said, 'Give me that mango,' moving her waist and hips.

'It's mine.' I heard myself say. They, too, were taken aback at my stance. I usually gave in, afraid of being beaten up. They looked at each other. Inez smiled. 'Give us all a bite then. One bite each.' That was an old trick; the fact that she felt she could use it again said a lot about her expectation of how little I would resist.

'No.' I said.

They were amused, knowing that together they could beat me into pulp. Then they stared at me, unbelieving, as torturers must do, at the obstinacy of a victim before the kill. They pressed in closer, their faces large and callous. Inez pushed me backwards and, as I tried to regain my balance, Millicent struck the mango from my clasp. It fell and rolled on the fine sand and then came to rest looking like a sand ball. They laughed and laughed. They pointed at it and could not contain their laughter. They pointed at me and moved backwards under the weight of their hilarity.

After they had gone, I knew that I couldn't leave the mango there in the yard. I walked up to it, picked it up and dropped it into a large open bin buzzing with flies. I went to one of the neat line of taps, washed my face and hands and sought privacy and shelter in the shade.

THE CINEMA

There were two cinemas in Tunapuna, the Palladium and the Monarch, the latter owned by the family of my late uncle, who had died, I learnt, in tragic circumstances. He, his wife and several children had lived in an upstairs house which was so large that it took grown-ups quite some time to walk from one end to the next. And there were so many rooms that visitors had been known to get lost.

One night the house caught fire and everyone (there were several maids to keep such a house gleaming) had rushed out as quickly as they could. When they were all safely outside the now fiercely burning building, my uncle asked his wife for their three month old baby. It was only then they realised he was still in his cot, each one thinking that the other had him.

My uncle rushed back into the rapidly burning building to look for the child. How he managed in that furnace to find his way through the various rooms to the right room and bring the child out, without any protective clothing, no one could say. It was said that he jumped from the first floor with the baby, for the steps had already gone. They were both burnt beyond recognition. In hospital, the baby died first and my uncle two days later.

The years passed by and a new house was built, as grand as the last, but my aunt did not recover from grieving for her husband and child.

My mother believed that business was business and should not be mixed with family sentiment and so, particularly since her brother's death, she insisted we should pay to get into my uncle's cinema. So I was always given the ticket money and an additional six cents to buy a packet of nuts. Occasionally, if any of my first cousins were collecting the tickets at the door, they would invite me to see the show for free. However, they were not often there, and there was no way of knowing in advance when they would be there, so, very rarely was I able to save my ticket money.

The cinema was the only form of entertainment Hindu girls enjoyed outside the festivities of their home and those of their wider family and community. I looked forward to the Sunday matinee show. There I saw African jungles, with elephants and crocodiles; Robin Hood and his merry men and the lovable fat Friar Tuck; knights in armour, like Ivanhoe; maidens in towers; kings and trumpets and the drawing up of bridges across castle moats. It was all exciting and magically different from the life around me. The idea of a moat appealed to me greatly.

And there was the lazy, glamorous American way of life: large cars, big-shot talk, smiling blondes and all that kissing, so public and so alien to my village life; and the grand panoramic spectacles of *The Robe* and *Quo Vadis* and *Samson and Delilah*. These films were discussed at length by the young men of the village who, in the absence of a village club, would while away long hours on the red iron railway swing-gate, watching the passers-by. Politics, football and cricket were popular subjects but the film *Samson and Delilah* evidently touched a tender spot, for after seeing it they spoke loudly, saying that women were not to be trusted and that though they had always known this, the extent to which it was true only came home to them after they had seen Delilah in action. Later, I realised how much this sentiment was being expressed for the benefit of us village girls.

Everything in the cinema was new, remote and unreal. It was like a magic box. Technicolour was sheer delight; it made the colours of the earth look as if they were fading and some gigantic smiling artist had given everything a fresh coat of paint: the grass and the moss on the stones in the river were greener; the straw in birds' nests was a more golden yellow; the aquamarine blue of the island seas was deeper; the scales of fish, like armour plate, were more glistening. Thatch and dusty ordinary roads, even the popular roses and the common hibiscus: all looked far more beautiful than I had imagined.

The fact that before and after the show, the screen was white, plain, motionless and empty, emphasised the cinema's unreality, like a magic carpet. But while irrelevant to life in the village, it fed my imagination. I was Tarzan whenever I was alone on a tree branch and Robin Hood too; the numbers of arrows I shot from my sheaf, strapped tightly behind my back, must have risen and fallen in their thousands.

But there were also the Indian religious films. What struck me in these were the snakes, so frequently used by gods and devils to test the faith of saints. It was their dappled spotted skin and inquiring, cautious glances which excited and paralysed me. The way they lifted their heads, as if each time they would decide afresh how much of their elongated self was neck, and their whiplike forked tongues have remained with me. There were other transformations – gods taking the form of stray dogs and beggars to test the faith of men – which made me look at these unfortunates differently.

But then Inez took away from me the pleasure of the cinema. I must have told her that my uncle owned the Monarch cinema and there and then she came up with the idea that I should give her the money my mother gave me for the cinema and I tell the ticket collector who I was.

I did not like the idea of going to the ticket collector and asking to be allowed in. But, after much thought, I reluctantly decided that I would ask my Aunt's permission to attend the cinema. What I was doing made me ashamed, but I had to choose between being bullied at school day after day or one afternoon of private humiliation. I was ten years old then and opted for the latter. How to go about it was the problem. I felt dishonest about using the pretext of a social call but there was also a deeper reason for my recoil.

When my Uncle was building his cinema many years ago, he had given my father full responsibility for almost everything to do with the construction, and with hindsight all agree that my father managed to build a fine cinema and had kept costs remarkably low. But as the project came to a close, both men, weary and tired, had a row and things were said on both sides that should not have been said. Years passed and though, after her brother's death, my mother kept a friendly contact with her sister-in-law and nephews and nieces, my father kept his distance. What he would have thought of this plan of mine, I have never wished to contemplate.

I told my mother that I was going to call on my aunt before I attended the matinee show. As my mother had given me the ticket money, and had no idea of my true intent, she welcomed this, asking me to give her regards and be sure to enquire after my aunt's health.

Inez was waiting for me at the Tunapuna market, which at half past three was no longer the colourful, bustling place it had been in the morning. Empty tables and boxes and rummaging dogs were the only witnesses to my handing over my money to Inez. I told her, more confidently than I felt, that I would join her later.

The iron gate to the grand house was not locked. When I pushed, it creaked like a crying child. The dogs began to howl and though they were tied with a chain I felt wretched. I suspected they had a sixth sense and knew why I was there.

This commotion brought out Dolly, the maid. 'Oh is you,' she said. I smiled broadly.

'Down Tiger,' she said. 'Down! Down, I tell you!' She turned to me 'You come to see *Mamee?*'

'Yes.'

'Come this way. The dogs frighten you na?'

'Yes.'

'We have to keep them; things bad round here and we don't have a man in the house; you understand?'

'Yes.'

'So how you keeping? Is a long time since I saw you. I don't think I saw you since the *katha*,' she said.

'How is *Mamee?*' I answered.

'She as usual. No better, no worse.'

Dolly brought me through several large rooms to a porch at the back of the house where my aunt was reclining in a hammock.

'How you, Mamee?'

'So so. And how is your mother? She well?'

'She alright, oui. She told me not to forget to ask you how you keeping.'

'Well I still the same way, no worse, thank God.'

'That's good.... How is Satrohan?'

'I don't know where he is. Dolly, you know where Satrohan is?'

'He was just here a minute ago. Satrohan!' Once more she called out his name, but no reply came.

'I see the roses doing very well,' I said.

'I don't know anything much about roses,' my aunt replied. 'The gardener is good with them.'

'Could I go out and look at them?'

'Go na. The only thing is – the dogs. If they see you in the garden they wouldn't rest. Dolly, hold the dogs; let Kamla see the roses.

'Not to worry, man; is too much trouble. I will see them from here.'

'From here? What can you see? Dolly, hold the dogs, let

72

Kamla see the roses.' Dolly did not move, and my aunt again said, 'Dolly, hold the dogs for Kamla.'

'Go Kamla, I will hold the dogs.'

I felt wretched. Here I was making overworked, tired Dolly stand out in the yard with the dogs, holding onto their collars, while I pretended to look at roses in the garden. The dogs wouldn't rest, and their howling accused me in the hushed Sunday afternoon. I looked at the roses. I concentrated on them. Some did cast a curious glance at me. I examined their thorns and wondered whether they knew why I was here, but I couldn't keep this up for long and soon returned to the porch. 'It is a very nice day,' I said. 'You should get a hammock built outside. On a day like this you should get the early morning sun.'

'I don't like the sun, you know, not at all. If I stay out in the sun just for one minute, one minute I tell you, I get one splitting headache. Ask Dolly.'

'Oh I'm so sorry to hear.'

'This is not something new. Since I was a child, the sun and I don't agree.'

'Oh I didn't know that,' I said, feeling more and more terrible. 'So how you otherwise?'

'I have a bad hip, the doctor told me to take things easy. I can't walk about. The minute I lift this foot just a little bit from the ground,' and she measured one inch with her forefinger, 'I get one pain, I tell you, like a needle going through me.' Then, I felt a hollow pause in the air, the sort of desolate emptiness that rests in dusty, abandoned ruins.

'How is your mother?' My aunt's voice seemed weary.

'She well up to now.'

'She is lucky. Anybody who have their health don't know how lucky they are.'

'That is true.'

Again that uncomfortable silence lay heavily. I felt awkward. How should I ask? I couldn't return home and tell my mother I'd decided not to see the show. An hour had passed. I knew the trailers would have started. I could hear the music coming from the cinema next door. Again that hollow silence hovered. I could not ask. I felt I had to leave.

It was Dolly – plain, ordinary, overworked Dolly – who came to my rescue. 'Why don't you go and see the show, Kamla?' she said.

'Is it good?' I asked.

'I don't know.'

'I'll go anyway,' I said, rather too hastily and before anyone could say anything. I was afraid my conservative aunt might not have approved of the film for children. Already halfway out of the porch I asked, 'Should I go round the side or the front?'

'The side door is closed now. You will have to pass in the front. Ask for Narine, tell him it's alright,' my aunt said.

When I entered the cinema it was dark; the trailers were still on: a good sword fight from *The Three Musketeers*. I sat down on the nearest chair and began to forget the roses, the dogs and Inez.

RED HOT ANTS

To the left of us there was the open savannah, but to the right was a substantial piece of land, unkempt and overgrown with clumps of pawpaw, a couple of coconut trees, lime trees and a castor oil tree with its leaves like wide open fingers. There was also a ramshackle barrack-house with three front doors in which three tenants lived. They had no inside kitchens and cooked their meals on a coalpot in the open unfloored space in front of their doors. Every passer-by knew what was being cooked.

I could not work out how they lived. Many weeks would pass and the houses would be deserted and then one day we would smell food being cooked, but after a few days of quiet solitary living, they would be off again, each going their separate ways. I had read about nomads in the desert; were these nomads of the suburbs?

One day a lady moved in with two children, Carl and Cynthia. They were older than I, but as they were left alone all day by their mother (they had no father, though a man wearing a jacket and a tie would very occasionally visit them) they would play marbles and hopscotch with me during the long August holidays. Although they were bigger and tougher and won most of the games, I continued to go over and play with them.

One afternoon they called me over, saying they had something to tell me. I was pleased to hear this and wondered what it might be. They were both standing at their front door.

'What is it?'

'Come closer,' they said.

'Why?'

'It's a secret. Come closer.'

I came closer until I was so close that any secret could have been safely shared.

'Tell me.' I said, beginning to feel suspicious. They ummed and aahhed until I was convinced, sure they had nothing to say.

'Go on,' I urged. 'What is it?'

It was then I felt a hot stinging pain on my feet, and when looked down I saw that I was standing on a nest of the dreaded bacchac ants, the warrior harvesters of equatorial forests, the cutters of leaves and bark. They were a burnished red, segmented, and vicious.

I stepped back and tried to brush them off with my hands but because of the pain and the numbers swarming upon me I ran screaming to my home; all this while both brother and sister laughed and laughed and danced their merriment.

I rushed home, opened the tap and put my feet under it. I allowed the water to flow on and on over my feet, but still they burned while Cynthia's and Carl's laughter pierced the air. I went inside, took a soft piece of white cotton cloth and comforted my feet. I anointed the many raised red bites with coconut oil. My eyes welled over and I asked myself Why? Why? Was this life? Why had they done this?

75

It might have been because my father owned two shops. I may have looked like someone easy to intimidate. Whatever it was, Monica began to extort money from me. She was much older than I; she was intelligent and forward, and had successfully guided her teachers to be well-disposed towards her. She played for high stakes. Every week she demanded that I give her six cents or else. I was able to put her off during the week but when Friday came I had to deliver. One Friday, she came up to me and said, 'Where is the money?' I tried to put her off further by saying that I had forgotten it at home and that if she wanted it, she would have to come there. She agreed to do so and I thought nothing would come of it.

To my surprise, she turned up at our front gate on that Sunday morning and asked to see me. I was confused. My mother said, 'Somebody at the gate to see you.' When I saw who it was, my heart sank and my stomach churned. I went to the shop, took six cents from the cash box and gave it to her. I felt so wretched, robbing my parents to protect my own skin and all because I didn't know how to cope with this kind of ugliness.

Afterwards my mother said, 'What she want?'

'She came to borrow a book but I realise I need it for my homework.'

My mother said nothing.

The following Friday when Monica again demanded: 'You bring it?' I said, 'Come Sunday.'

On this occasion when she came to our front gate, my mother and I were sitting together shelling pigeon peas. My mother could see her as she was sitting on the threshold of the kitchen door but I was hidden from Monica by the kitchen wall. My mother said: 'That girl is back again.' Without any thought or plan I heard myself say: 'She has come for money. She's always pestering me for money and says that if I don't give her she will beat me up. She's one of a gang at school.'

My mother said, 'Oooh, is that it. Coming here for money, encouraging you to steal.' She got up from the *peerha* and walked calmly to the gate as if she was merely going outside to do her customary weeding of our pathway.

I heard only snippets of what my mother was saying: 'Will tell your mother and the Headmaster. ...will have to call the police. I know where you live, I know that area well. ...jail .... the court house... encouraging those younger than yourself to steal.,... punishable in law.'

To my surprise I heard Monica denying that she had come for money so strongly and convincingly that even I wondered whether, on this occasion, she had perhaps wanted something different. But my mother was more experienced than I and was not taken in. I heard repeatedly, several words and phrases as, jail... will complain to your parents... the police will be coming round to you, mark my word, if this continues.'

When my mother came back at last, I felt a great relief. It was as if I had been entombed and suddenly the doors of the heavy vaults were opening of their own accord.

All day Sunday I felt calm. On Monday morning, however, as I got ready for school, I began to wonder whether Monica would be waiting for me with the rest of the gang. As I crossed the railway line and did not see any of them standing in front of the school gate, I felt that perhaps they were hiding behind it, the better to surprise me. I looked through the crevice between the hinges but they were not there.

I walked to my classroom as if it were the path to the guillotine and stood and waited for the surprise attack. I placed my books in the desk and walked away to the back yard. The gang was not there. For the entire day I moved with an expectation of the worst at any moment. But nothing happened on that day or the next or the next. It was my last term at Tunapuna Government Primary School and when I did leave, I never met any member of the gang again; they just disappeared as nightmares do when you wake.

PART THREE

AWAKENING

PASEA VILLAGE

At dusk it was easy to believe you were in India: shadows and sounds of bullock carts, the aroma of *roties* on *chulhas;* fresh water in buckets and cut grass in bales; off-white houses with thatched roofs and glowing wood fires in the yards; the soft gentle sound of Hindi in the night carried by warm winds along red earth tracks. Even as late as the 1930s it was easy to believe.

In 1890 my grandfather, a babe in arms, was taken off the ship by his mother. It is difficult to know what these new arrivals expected to find, but after many weary, fearful months at sea, where the toll from sickness and disease was sometimes as high as a quarter or more, to disembark, to set foot on land, would have brought some comfort to these indentured labourers, many of whom had never seen the wide open ocean before.

They came to work in sugarcane fields and sugar factories. They came to work under men who were once owners of slaves and for men who believed in their own inherent superiority before God and before man, but most of all before colonised men and women. It was a period of still unbridled British apartheid.

Whatever harshness these labouring men and women endured, and there was much, by the early 1940s their children and grandchildren, born during the long humiliating period of contract labour, did not speak of it. Instead, all hopes were set on what blessings tomorrow would bring, if one worked ceaselessly, from dawn to dusk in the fields and from dusk to deepest night at home. They built their homes with competence and skill from cool, soothing materials: earth and dried grass held together by a skeletal frame of strong slender wood. When a house was built, neighbours heaved shoulder to shoulder. The walls were smoothed down and finally painted over with a lime mixture which gave them that peaceful off-white calm. Straw-coloured roofs, simple wooden doors and windows and beams darkened by wood smoke, were made cool by siting the houses in the path of the prevailing wind and by having verandahs on the east and or the west; comfort was created by erecting wooden shelves wherever they were needed.

Between the beams and the thatched roof were secret places for hiding money, jewellery and important papers. Other things – good vegetable seeds, tobacco and rum – had their special places of safekeeping too. There were the visibles – a horse's bridle, saddle and harness and strong rope, sharp knives and garden tools – all hanging from strong nails under rafters. Every corner of these houses was made use of. There were no special rooms, no such thing as a guest room. There was no space allocated to the make-believe of something better than their situation allowed. The day-to-day comforts of the family were the same for visiting relatives. During harvest time tomatoes were ripened under the high four-poster iron bed and pumpkins and melongenes were stored there too, or in sheltered cool corners of any room.

The large open yards were shielded from outside eyes by strong thick hibiscus hedges, the stems of which were chewed and used as tooth brushes. There were fruit trees: star-apple, sapodilla, soursop, pawpaw, plums, chennet; avocados as large as coconuts with the flavour of the finest, freshest, home-made country butter; and mangoes: rose mango, starch mango, doux douce, box and spice and Julie mango. And one must not forget the common long mango which gives a lot of shade and cools the surrounding air, while being the best variety for making *kutchala* and *achar* stored in large glass jars or enormous earthen russet coloured ones and left in the sun to mature. It was easy for me to imagine men hiding in jars when I read the Arabian tales of *A Thousand and One Nights*.

In larger yards there would be a tamarind tree, coconuts, a variety of bananas and 'figs' – 'silk figs' and 'sucre figs' – oranges, grapefruits and shaddock and a shataigne or bread nut tree.

(The latter, when ripe, provides an edible sweet nut that is first boiled in salted water. When still green the meat of this large hanging fruit is a tasty vegetable.) At the back of the houses there were neat vegetable gardens, usually of spinach, melongene, beans, tomatoes and vines of pumpkin and squash. Pigeon peas were planted in straight lines along the boundary of plots, looking like friendly sentinels in the breeze.

But to me the *machan* was the most fascinating, simple and effective idea in vegetable growing. The *machan* was a high platform made of bamboo on which a variety of vines were encouraged to curl themselves and run miles and miles on one spot, so enabling cucumbers, *keraila* and a wide variety of beans to flourish. It was a practical and clever way of making maximum use of limited space. Bamboo screens or wire mesh screens also served as wind breaks.

Most people cooked with wood brought in trucks from the forest. The villagers made their own fireside or *chulha* for cooking. Each *chulha* had characteristics that were tailored to the individual home. We had two: one just outside the kitchen steps in the yard, used in the dry season, and the other inside. My mother first constructed a raised platform in the kitchen and then built on it her *chulha*, strengthened with bricks and stones before it was plastered over with a mix of earth, cow manure and lime. Because it had been built in this way, she did not have to stoop or bend when cooking. The fireside had openings for four pots at any one time. The circumference of the openings varied to accommodate pots with large, small and medium bottoms.

During the dry season when almost anything could be used as fuel – coconut shells or corn husks – women cooked outside. It was a sensory delight to walk slowly in the dusk on the main Pasea road when evening meals were being prepared. The women busily darting in and out of their kitchens were probably oblivious to the pleasures I received from the rich warm aroma of wood-smoke, *roties* lifting themselves from hot iron tawas, vegetables in *massala*, fried fish and the intoxicating smell of warm roasted spices – *jeera, methi,* chili, and garlic. These flavours comforted and energised me, as one aroma mingled with another, so that by the time I arrived home I was in a more than ready state for my evening meal.

Although we had piped and metered water in our yard for as far back as I can remember, before the 1940s there was no piped water inside the houses and few people had piped water in their yards. Instead there were 'stand pipes' with round brass heads which had to be pressed on with all one's strength before the 'government water' flowed. People got round that by holding a heavy rock on the round yellow metal head. Later, the easier turn-on taps were introduced. Then men would bathe there, though keeping on their old khaki short trousers so as not to arouse the disapproval of the village elders, for this was a hard-working, no-nonsense, conservative society. Our road was well served with three standpipes about 200 yards apart. Mothers bathed their children there and occasionally, on a Sunday, I saw men scrubbing down their horses.

The unpaved roads were made of lateritic clay and the hollows, spherical in shape and plum in the middle, were carved out by cart wheels. When the clods of clay and gravel cracked and the bullock carts pounded them into dust, one was overpowered by this choking, whirling dust picked up by the strong Trade Winds.

In the rainy season the roads became a bright sea of shallow reddish, yellowish pools complete with gleefully sporting tadpoles. I knew the width and length of the pond in front of our shop but heaven help a stranger at night without a torchlight! When we had a good downpour the open drains gave up and the road became a stream with fast-moving tributaries fanning out to the left and to the right. Some sections of our roads became better suited to Irish corries than pedestrians. Then well dressed women had to remove their *chappals,* lift their skirts, though no higher than a tolerable mid-calf, and wade through. On such occasions a passing bullock cart was a gift from the gods.

When the rains went away, there were the two large

savannahs to enjoy, with their mature trees which spread out leafy branches and provided shelter from the piercing fierceness of the noonday sun and rest for all living things: the countless butterflies and birds and dragonflies.

There was the high railway embankment to escape to, where I often sat, barefoot, hair dishevelled, my clothes sequined with prickly seeds, waiting for the trains, the huge, shining black steam engines which would hisss and pussssscchhh on arrival and departure, singing loud and clear the same song, 'Chocolate water killed meh daughter, chocolate water killed meh daughter.' Well, that's what my mother said. I listened intently several times and found that she was right. I was seldom alone. Wild flowers, strange-smelling medicinal plants and flowering weeds and butterflies kept me company and sometimes there was a gang of boys who joined me uninvited.

Like conspirators we camouflaged our true intent. We would wave to everyone on the train and this pleased the engine driver and his mate, the passengers and the lonely fellow in the railway van attached to the last carriage. But as soon as the train passed by we scrambled down to examine whether our crown corks, roughly flattened by hand, had now attained that final stage of perfection: flatness, smoothness, thinness and sharpness. For when a perfect spinner spins, harnessed by two holes and thin strong marlin, it sings and dances fast; loses its tin quality and in its whirling motion meshes into the blue sky, becoming one with it, a delight to the possessor and a source of envy to onlookers.

It was our delight too to play 'hoop' (hide-and-seek) in the late afternoon during those short tropical twilights, and see our shadows tower high over walls and fences and scale them like giants with ease, and to be then ever watchful for silent clues: the shadow of an unwary playmate.

But many of these village things have gone. For my family it all began on that night the sun visited us. Of the entire village – only us. My father had paid for its carriage and our home was made ready. We were excited but not prepared for its naked harsh intensity, its yellowish white brilliance. It dazzled our eyes and we sheltered them, observing with childlike pleasure and wonder that the once black, impenetrable yard could now be seen. Meanwhile, unnoticed, the shadows within our rooms had fled and though it was well past six, it seemed like the sun had stayed the night.

Electric lights had come.

It started simply with a hole in the ground and a planted pole. It was straight and erect and sturdy and for many months it stood alone. Then two men came and attached wires to it from the town across the railway line. Much later still, two other men came and connected our house to wires leading from the pole. We were the first to have electric lights in the village because my father was able to pay the government fifty dollars for an electric pole.

To me it was sheer magic – the swiftness with which an entire room was lit up. And so, for the very last time, my mother washed the lampshades and put them away safely – 'Just in case,' she said.

Gone was the morning ritual of bringing the lamps out from each room, trimming their wicks, adding more oil, washing lamp shades and allowing them to drip dry. Gone were the rituals of twilight when, as the sun sank behind the horizon, my mother would say her evening prayer before she lit the first lamp. Only after this could the other lamps in the house be lit; often Daya, impatient to close her day's work and not wishing to light the lamps before my mother's evening prayers, had to send me to remind her of her duty.

In the days of lamps there were shadows that were alive and bouncing: a shirt, a pyjama resting on a nail, a tall sock, a tie, a belt, a basket or a hat, hanging where only a flicker of light penetrated, were magically transformed with an energy, a personality (at times threatening) and a power they did not possess by day.

And before the coming of street lights there was something sombre and moving about standing by the wayside watching the incoming bullock carts loaded with bales of grass and baskets of vegetables, the lanterns and flambeaux flickering on the tired faces and rested thoughts of men and women coming from the fields.

But there was also the challenge of trying to hop on the back of an open cart for a ride, even for just a few yards down the road, without arousing the anger of the driver holding the long whip; then there would be the triumph of hailing out to passers-by while perched aloft on the cart. Later I felt this pleasure so keenly that I likened it to the joys of the Queen of Sheba floating down the Nile.

And later too I felt that not having electric lights had another sound blessing, for, in the absence of electric poles, we had uninterrupted freedom of the skies during the kite-flying season. But when electricity came to the village, kites and their long cloth tails were caught on the high wires, forever dangling, whirling and whirring as seasons came and went. And just as the carcass of a splendid bird bleaches and withers until passers-by ask, 'What was it that died there?', so too, our captured kites, our giant flamboyant, mad bulls of the air, once free, once our great pride, dancing sinuously with gold and silver streamers, humming in the sky, provoking the clouds, with time, became tangled, tattered knots and passers-by said, 'What a miserable sight! Why don't we clean up those wires?'

MRS. ROJAS AND HER JULIE MANGOES

Nearly everyone in Pasea was Indian, except for a few black people who lived mainly on our road, and the white overseer, Mr. Rojas and his wife. They lived in a large rectangular wooden house with a sign on the gate: 'Beware of the dog.' What Mr. Rojas actually oversaw, we village children could not say, for we saw little of him. Mrs. Rojas was plump but not friendly. I don't believe she was unfriendly by nature; simply, she had no one to show her how to smile. Here she was in this huge rambling house with a large verandah at the front and back, a frightened maid, a parrot, no children, few callers and two quite vicious dogs; and Mr. Rojas who did not hear well and walked with his head bent to negotiate the puddles in the rainy season and the cow pats in the dry.

But Mrs. Rojas had those special grafted mangoes to sell, the Julie mango, which now reigns supreme as the queen of mangoes. She would put on her gate a little notice scrawled in a bad hand: 'fresh Julie mangoes call'. You had to call out very loudly because she could be anywhere in that large house. 'Good morning! Good morning!' we would shout. There would usually be at least five of us; there was courage in numbers. Sometimes we would vary our call to a 'yuhooo' since that sound was carried by the wind.

While we talked of the sweet pleasures soon to be enjoyed, two dogs would appear as if from nowhere, hounds harnessed to the Furies, rushing through the air towards us innocent village callers. In the past our first reaction was to give ourselves a head start before they could reach the gates; later we realised that the gate itself was our shield, having tested it for strength, so we held our ground.

'Grrrrr ow; ow ow ow. Grrrrr...' two unfriendly dogs growled. After a while Mrs. Rojas appeared, often looking as if we had woken her from a much needed sleep.

She addressed the dogs first:

'Jacob and Solomon, come here.'

The dogs pointed to us eagerly with their mouths, delighted they had discovered us. They enacted this denouncement twice, the second time with their heads, making sure our presence was recognised by their mistress. When they were satisfied that Mrs. Rojas had seen us, they ran up to her and stood guard.

'Silly dogs!' I think.

'What you want?' she growled.

'Mangoes.'

'You have money?'

'Yes.'

'How much?' Faced with this question we were never sure how to accommodate our needs, our means; and the truth.

'You have any bird-pecked ones?' Carmen would ask; she had a wiliness greater than most grown ups. Mrs. Rojas was quite happy to sell bird-pecked mangoes in her back verandah to the village children, but she did not want it to get further than them.

'I don't have bird-pecked ones.' We would look enquiringly at her. We had all the time in the world. 'Come in all the same,' she would finally say, seeing that the road was clear.

All five of us moved in like young buccaneers. We followed her to the back verandah. There was nothing on the table.

'Mary,' she called out, 'bring the red tray.' Meantime we looked at her neat orchard of Julie mangoes. They were well within our reach. Then Mary, a thin black girl with a clean, starched and ironed white apron and a white cap, came in slowly with the tray. Mrs. Rojas studied it. 'There is one missing,' she accused.

In the meantime all of us had the same fruitful idea of investigating the possibilities of a back entrance to this orchard of delights.

'I did not check them, Madam.'

'But I did,' retorted Mrs. Rojas. There was an awkward silence and both ladies looked at each other as though fencing with their eyes.

'Oh alright,' Mrs. Rojas conceded and Mary left.

On the tray there were bird-pecked mangoes, some pecked in one place, others in two. The circumference of the pecks varied, but someone had carefully separated bird pecks of a small circumference from, bird pecks of a larger. We looked at this neat handiwork.

'How much you have?' she queried.

We had one penny each and could only get two with ten cents. It couldn't be done; there were five of us. We had wasted her time, she complained. We closed the gate behind us and sat by the roadside and agreed how easy it would be to enter from the back were it not for those vicious silly dogs.

Some may think that because the Pasea villagers were East Indians there was amongst them a uniformity of colour and culture. What we had, in reality, was a mosaic of peoples: Moslems who would not eat pork but would eat beef and who distrusted Hindus, and we Hindus who ate neither and distrusted the Moslems. There were also the short dark Madrassis and the ivory-coloured Brahmins from Northern India, tall, well-proportioned people with features like those of the gods and goddesses hanging on our walls. People came in all shapes and sizes: women tall and slender as grains of Basmati rice; some pear-shaped; others like the figure eight. There were men who walked with slow comfortable steps, lazy stomachs and greedy eyes and others who were lean and bronzed, walking spindles of energy, for whom all things were possible.

There was, of course, this matter of religion.

Moslems were not invited to our *kathas* and *pujas* and we were not invited to their mosques. So side by side we walked the dirt roads not knowing anything about the deeper feelings of the other. This was brought home to me when after repeated invitations my mother failed yet again to persuade our Moslem neighbour, Mrs. Hassan, to a friendly get-together.

'Would you come and eat with me?' Mrs. Hassan challenged my mother one day in the shop, tired of my mother's persistence. My mother had asked her: 'Tell me, is it that you don't like our style of cooking? Is it something we use in our food that does not agree with you?' At first, Mrs. Hassan had smiled and, as in the past, dismissed the question with, 'I'm so busy. Where will I find the time to eat out? Do you know how much I have to do?'

My mother pretended not to hear and repeated, 'Tell me, I wouldn't take offence. If you don't tell me what it is, I will never know, because I'm not a mind reader.' It was then that Mrs. Hassan had challenged my mother with her question, 'Would you come and eat with me?'

'Why yes,' my mother said.

'You are only saying that. I know better.'

'Why wouldn't I come?'

'You too smart, Maharajin.'

'No! No! You must tell me why I wouldn't come. If you invite me I will come. Look we have three people here in the shop as witnesses. I tell them and I tell you, if you invite me I will come.' Challenged so directly, Mrs. Hassan was embarrassed and left the shop quietly with her goods.

The next day at about two in the afternoon, when most people who had a choice were sleeping or resting quietly, Mrs. Hassan came. My mother was weighing and parcelling out flour in five-pound paper bags to make things easier for her when the shop got busier.

'You see,' she said, 'we kill our chicken and our goat in a special way. Prayers have to be said and animals have to be killed in a prescribed way laid down in the *Koran*. I cannot eat if the animal is not killed in a certain way.'

'I say prayers too. I always say prayers before I kill the hens and I always give them a drink of water.'

'It is not the same, Maharajin.'

'Alright. Who kills the chicken in your home?' My mother asked.

'What you mean?'

'Do the children's father kill the chicken at you?'

'No! No! No! You don't understand, you don't have to be a man, any Moslem can do it.'

'Good. That is all I want to hear. Now this Sunday I will send Kamla for you, and you will come and kill the chickens. I could ask Hamid next door to do it but you might still have doubts in your mind, so the best thing is, for you to come and do it.' That Sunday Mrs. Hassan came over and killed four chickens 'her way'. My mother asked me not to 'hang about her' as she might require privacy. And so it was that from then on we had a happy and more relaxed Mrs. Hassan who occasionally accepted our invitation, and from time to time sent us a bowl of vermicelli boiled in milk and sugar and spices.

Christmas was the one festivity everybody in the village celebrated. Hindus, Moslems and Christians all planned what they were going to do for Christmas with equal fervour.

A month before Christmas my mother sent a message to George. He was fat and jolly and talked, walked and worked in a way that would have made a snail a front runner.

'I believe in taking meh time. All this rushing about doesn't agree with meh system and I talking from long hard experience. Not good for the heart. You don't believe me? Well, you ask the doctor.' He introduced himself that way to people he did not know; we who knew him called him 'the slow boat to China.'

He came to give our salmon-pink walls a new coat of paint and when he left he always said, 'You go have a good Xmas now, look at them walls pretty foh so.'

But it was only when my elder sister moved into third gear that I knew Christmas was close ahead. She roped in anyone she could find to assist her in what was truly a Herculean task; whether they were busy people like Daya and Renee or the village boys skylarking about in front of our shop or idling away their time on the railway crossing gate. She would give the boys a heavy wooden dining chair and a piece of sandpaper to remove last year's varnish and kept a close eye on what they were doing.

As a very young child I was given the job of taking the salt out of the rich reddish Norwegian cooking butter that came to Trinidad in large tins. It was a laborious task and my sister was very particular. Table butter was generally not available and was expensive. So after a number of stirs of 'washing the butter' with clean tap water, the salted water was drained off and fresh water added. It took almost a whole half day to wash the butter to my sister's satisfaction.

As I got older I helped with the sandpapering, polishing and varnishing. But as my father's hardware store on the Tunapuna Eastern Main Road grew, my youngest brother and I were recruited to the permanent staff during our Christmas holidays. It was hard work being on one's feet all day. Shops opened at eight in the morning and closed twelve hours later. We were given time off for a quick lunch, but I seldom got home before half-past eight at night.

We sold paints: paints for wood, for enamel and for walls; mahogany, rosewood and clear varnish; dyes and brushes – all sorts; linseed oil, turpentine, nails and hammers; polish and sandpaper – all grades.

It was a busy time, made more hectic by the annual conspiracy villagers and town people entered in – to leave every possible thing for the last minute. We also sold toys: dolls and trains and large brightly coloured spinning-tops so popular with younger children. The more expensive gifts were in boxes, the less expensive ones in plastic bags. There were other fast-moving Christmas goods: curtain materials, oilcloths and linoleum. Though we called it a hardware store, it was in truth a general store.

Christmas Eve night was the grand finale: all the domestic toil of the past weeks came to a crescendo. It was a night when our home was not merely transformed; it became a joy. In a quiet mysterious way the old ordinary things acquired a magic, an enchantment. Take our kitchen safe: the old wooden safe that no-one noticed had disappeared and in its place was a safe of deep rosewood that beamed and sparkled and captured laughing eyes like a mirror.

It was the moment when everything, from the brass on the four-poster bed to the hat rack in the corridor, took on a state as near perfection as it was possible to achieve. Whether the wide satin bows which gathered the curtains, the gold-fringed lace which charmed our beds into becoming airborne chariots, the fine brocade bed covers or the embroidered pillow cases: everything was as it should be. Every item of furniture smelt cared for, given a new lease of life with oils, varnish or polish.

On the kitchen floor there was a new piece of linoleum; on the dining table a new oilcloth with patterns of bunches of grapes and pears and peaches all miraculously on one vine.

The wooden floors had been scrubbed, the kitchen walls painted with an emulsion and every cupboard had had its contents removed, dusted or washed, and its shelves given a new lining of satin-smooth cream paper.

It was not merely the cleanliness but the feeling of space around everything which was so satisfying. It was the feeling that light was now penetrating into the furthest corner, unimpeded by the day-to-day accumulation of trivia and clutter. No matter where the eye roamed, one was met by beauty and affection, by signs of human care. All this had been brought about by the high standards set by my mother and followed by her family and by all whom she employed.

Christmas eve was a feast of exotic aromas. The moment you opened the outside gate to the house and walked into the open gallery, you did not want to have a shower and change, instead, you walked up to the wire-mesh food safe. There you would see through the fine metallic weave the most delicate, softest lemon cake made for us children, and, for the adults, a rich, moist, treacle-coloured fruit cake made of sultanas and raisins and currants and prunes which had been soaked in rum for two months. This cake would make visiting friends and relatives lift their heads and appeal to the gods – 'My god, this is champion!' – giving praise with their lips and eyes.

There were bottles of cashew nuts and large peanuts; freshly baked white bread and sweet bread made with fruit and nuts and ginger. There were home-made ginger ale and cherry brandy and, on the table beside a most elegant, patterned glass cakestand (supporting a perfect cake waiting to be cut), red wine in a frosted decanter.

Daya had left long ago but the tender roasted turkey, with its fresh herb and liver stuffing which she had cooked, would be there, covered securely from the cat. We were expected to help ourselves to it and the home-made bread.

What made Christmas eve night such an enchantment was that for the first time I had the leisure to see, to absorb and to wonder at the work my elder sister, Daya and Renee, the village boys, my mother and her neighbourly friends, had all contributed.

It was easy to believe I was at peace with myself, after I had showered and supped and sat on sweet-smelling cushion covers, with a piece of lemon cake in my hand, embraced by french-polished arms and by children's voices coming from the radio singing, 'Joy to the world the Lord has come'. In such a frame of mind I would pretend I was sitting instead somewhere inside one of those newly passe-partout-framed pictures, taken from a calendar, of Norwegian or Canadian mountains and forests and lakes and streams, which my sister had hung on the walls.

But there was another side to Christmas, a side I encountered one Christmas Eve night.

I have already said that stores and shops closed at eight at night. Christmas Eve was no different. This fact was well known. Nevertheless, there were always people who would rush in at the twelfth hour because they had forgotten to get something. From time to time someone would knock at the closed door pleading to be let in. If you were caught by the police selling after eight you could be charged. That was the law.

One of those instances I remember well.

Her face was streaming with perspiration when I saw her. It was clear that she had been running; she was gasping for breath and puffing. Her knock had been forceful and urgent and my father asked one of the clerks to see who it was.

'I want to speak to Ram,' the voice said.

'We are closed now,' the senior clerk replied from within.

'I know that, but I want to speak to the Boss.'

'Let her in,' my father said.

She stood before my father's heavy mahogany desk trying to calm her breathing. Perspiration streamed from her. She was busily wiping her face with a tightly squeezed, flowered handkerchief. When she came into the light I saw how great was her anxiety and stress.

'The lady I working with just let me off and I only just got paid. I haven't got anything for my little girl. I want a doll, only a doll.' My father, seated at his desk, nodded to her.

'See if you can help this lady,' he said, pointing to me.

We had sold all our dolls. Only one was left and that was because its leg had been broken from the thigh. I did not know what to say to her. She was clenching her money. There was one perfect doll but it was very expensive and for that reason it had not been bought. I could see she could not afford it and I decided not to mention it.

My father paid his staff and gave them Christmas presents of wines and spirits from his rum shop. They departed smiling. My younger brother and I were left with this lady. We also were tired and would have preferred to be on our way. 'We don't have any more dolls,' I said.

'No man, that isn't true.'

'Dolls were popular this year,' I replied.

'You know, I wanted to come at midday, but you know how it is when you working for white people. The pay is good, but I tell you child, you work for it.' There was a pause in which we looked at each other. 'You mean you don't have a single doll left? How can I tell Debbie that? You know I have to leave her with a friend. I promised her. You can't do me that. Have a look in the stock room for me na, you never can tell.'

I began to understand her situation. It was hopeless. 'There is only one doll left but...' and I rummaged through the soft white transparent paper of the empty large box. 'There you see, that is all.' I brought out the sad neglected doll without a leg.

'Is that all?'

'Yes.'

'Na man, have another look through. You never can tell.'

My feet were killing me and I sat down.

'Look Madam,' I said; 'believe me when I say, if we had fifty more dolls today, they would have been sold.' The doll could close and open her eyes and she had red hair. She kept staring at me.

'Is that all you have?'

'Yes.' My God, I thought, she is asking me the same question over and over again. She looked at me. By this time she had removed the money from her tightly clenched fingers to a small purse which she placed in her generous bosoms Both her hands were now more relaxed.

'Where is the leg?' she asked.

'I don't know,' I said, and that was the truth. To my surprise she started to laugh in a contagious way. 'I just can't believe this,' she said. 'You going to sell me a one-legged baby doll?'

My younger brother joined us; he brought a lovely red engine with an attractive black funnel. 'You can have this,' he said, 'I'm not charging you for it. It no longer winds up you see; but look at that engine! It's really heavy and strong and it runs.' He gave it a good push and it went hurrying on.

'You two are Ram's children, I can see that.'

'I'm not charging you for it,' he said.

'And I should hope not,' she answered, perking up. My brother wrapped it up and left.

The lady knelt down beside the box and began rummaging again. There was so much paper in it I decided I must help her. I got up and removed a substantial amount.

'There!' she said smiling, showing me the leg.

'You are lucky.'

'God is good,' she said. 'He looks after those who trust in him.' She paused and then said, 'How much?'

'I will have to ask my father.'

That night I soaked my feet in hot water for half an hour, caressed them with a cool, comforting white towel, massaged them with cold cream and sat down in the magic of our sitting room. I lit one of the old-fashioned lamps and took the electric lights off and there, in the flickering soft shadows, I sat quietly and absorbed all the goodness that was around me.

I remembered when she came to the desk with the doll and said, 'How much, Ram?'

My father said, 'I can't sell you a broken item, Madam. It is against the law.'

'So I can have it then.'

'If you want it you can have it. My son has offered you an

engine that has lost its winder. You are not having a good Christmas are you?'

'Well,' she said, 'what to do? You have to trust in God.'

'Yes.' My father said, and he put in the bag a handful of balloons, a 1945 calendar and a bottle of cherry brandy.

'God bless you,' she said, and as I opened the narrow door, we lost her to the night.

CHASTITY AND ADULTERY

Our village was a relatively calm place. There was the occasional row over a missing chicken, or undisciplined hens laying outside the reach of the hand that fed them. There were stick-fight contests where one of the participants could be badly hurt. On Saturday nights a few men became drunk and would sing all the way home, becoming overly-friendly to anyone they met. But they were harmless and there was always someone who would help them to get home safely.

No one stole from another, though front doors were not locked and most people left their homes to work their rice and vegetable plots some distance away. Our roads were safe for children and the old both during the day and at night.

But adultery was another matter. If committed by a wife, it was her death sentence if not physically, certainly socially. So too was premarital pregnancy – 'because of the "shame" it brought to the father of such an uncaring and foolish daughter. Never again could the father, the head of the house, be able to walk the road with his head held high.' That was how my grandmother had put it to me. There were few daughters who could cope with the silent persecution from their own village friends as well as from their immediate family. In the few instances in our village when youthful passion overleapt cultural barriers, the wrath of the father fell on the mother. She was ultimately held responsible for what was perceived as the imperfections in her daughter's upbringing and character. How a young lady ought to conduct herself was made clear to me in this story my mother told me – the story of Draupadi from the *Mahabharata*.

In the dark age, in the epoch of Dwapar, at Hastina-pura, there lived a young lady of great beauty called Draupadi who was about to have her nakedness revealed in the pavilion of the king's court by the courtier Dur-yodhana. He was full of his own importance and enraged that the enchanting Draupadi had repulsed his advances. Thus, overcome by unbridled desire, he held the loose end of her saris and began to undress her by pulling at it with demonic energy. The young Draupadi seeing that she was no match for this fierce courtier cried out to the heavens and appealed to Lord Krishna to come to her rescue. The bemused courtier scoffed at her naivety and with smiling lips and burning eyes began to unwrap her loveliness. Her soft silk sari glided through his arrogant fingers as he pulled and pulled – and the more his desire grew the more he pulled – and as he pulled, yards and yards of silk passed through his now moist fingers. And yet Draupadi was covered. How long he persisted at this devilish act I cannot says except to point out that when he fell exhausted to the ground, there was a high mountain of the softes,t strongest silk behind him and a fully-clothed, beautifully-chaste Draupadi before him.

Such stories affected me greatly and brought my mother and I closer together, and though in later years I realised that she had taken the material of many stories from the *Ramayana* and the *Mahabharata* and with a sculptor's chisel shaped them to her own liking, it was always done with the affection of a mother trying to impart a deeper wisdom to her naive, fast-growing daughter.

As the years rolled on, I could not help thinking that such tales had little effect on men. This may have been because adultery committed by men had a lot going for it, since it was seen as 'the way of men', one of the crosses wives had to bear with stoic calmness. That, I felt, was unfair and unjust. And I saw women's acceptance of this not as a result of their having a greater capacity to absorb pain or to forgive, as older women believed, but because of their helpless dependence upon their husbands. I was overcome by a deep sorrow for my sex in bondage, and for the real and terrifying predicament biology and custom had placed them in. I was not aware of how strongly I carried this sense of injustice until one day, after hearing of the ungracious behaviour of someone we all knew well, whose wife, a gentle soul, had shared her grief with my mother, I was startled to hear myself say: 'Men who commit adultery should be shot.' My father was much taken aback by the intensity of my wrath and looked at me rather strangely; such vehemence was uncalled for, he must have felt, for he quietly walked away. On his leaving, my mother said, 'You should show more regard and respect for your father's presence; you are not behaving as a daughter should. You are going out of step.'

Hindus, unlike Moslems, are not allowed more than one wife. Yet the Hindu epics tell of kings with many wives. Rama, one of the avatars of God, was the offspring of the third wife of King Dasharatha; while another reincarnation of God, Lord Krishna, appears to have enjoyed playing mischievous pranks with the ladies of the court: removing their clothes from the river bank while they bathed in the stream. I was never happy with this and felt that gods ought to conduct themselves differently.

In Tulsidas's retelling of Valmiki's *Ramayana,* there is an episode where Sita, wife of Rama, has just been freed by the capture of Lanka, and the death of the powerful king Ravana who has kept her captive. It has to be proved publicly that Sita has been faithful to her husband in both thought and deed. So she is put through what my mother described as her 'trial by fire', 'the proving of her purity' by the cleansing ritual of fire which consumes all human ugliness, including woman's unfaithfulness. Dressed in ochre robes, the colour of the ascetic, Sita enters the flames. The writer of this moving epic, I noted, allowed no extenuating circumstance whatever, for the woman. It was only when Sita stepped out of the fire, without a hair of her body singed, that she was able to return to her husband, Rama. Young Hindu girls like myself, aged eight when I first heard this story, enjoyed the rich imagery and poetry of these epic adventures, without being aware that we were unconsciously absorbing the sentiment and values of Valmiki. And so it was that I, too, was absorbed into that ancient tradition of storytelling and felt a close bond with tales that were written nearly three thousand years ago and handed down from mother to daughter ever since.

But as I became taller, my inner voice grew too, and one night, as I walked home with my mother from the cinema where I had just seen Sita put through this ordeal of fire, I asked: 'If Rama was God, shouldn't he have known that Sita was faithful? Didn't he trust her word?'

'Lord Rama had faith in his wife,' my mother replied, 'and did not feel the need for this public ritual, but you should remember Sita was returning from a long stay in the enemy's court to reign as queen over the people of Ayodha. Ravana was no ordinary man, he would have courted her with very many subtle allurements. There must be no blemish, not the slightest doubt, in the minds of any of her subjects – for there will always be doubters – that she was fit to be their Queen.'

Although I was not happy with this answer, I did not know how to oppose it. I could not come to terms with this trial by fire. My mother, seeing my uneasiness, said: 'You must remember, Kamla, that as queen she held a position of responsibility and of trust. All wives hold positions of great trust.'

'Do husbands hold positions of trust?' I provoked.

'Of course they do, there is no question about that.'

So it was that my understanding of morality was formed – by the interpretation of the *Ramayana* by my mother and by my father and the pundit and others, as you will see.

Thin, tall, hard-working, Tara was never sent to school, but she was equipped with that rare, valuable understanding called common-sense. All day she worked in the Tunapuna market, selling fruit, vegetables and ground provisions. Though she had a serious businesslike side to her, which she needed to help her gentle, quiet husband support their two sons and two daughters, she smiled a great deal and had much to say to us young people who lived close to her.

One morning, when I was dragging my feet on my way to primary school and wishing the school would disappear before I arrived, I met Tara on her way to the market. Observing my disposition, she rested her burden on the road and said, 'Look at me, you want to work hard like this?' pointing to the heavy basket of *baigan, karaili* and *bodi*. 'No child, study hard at school and trust in God.' And she smiled, 'Who knows? You may one day become a doctor, a lawyer, banker. Who knows? Once you set your mind on something there is nothing, nothing at all to stop you. But trust in God and ask him for his blessings. When you have that, no man can stop you.'

When the Tunapuna market closed at half-past four, Tara came home and did whatever housework, yardwork and shopwork there was to do. Her husband and children helped but Tara was like a merry-go-round, here one minute, there another; always working. I couldn't help feeling that even when she was in her outdoor bathroom she would be diligently using her pumice stone, rubbing herself. But what came through in all her transactions, whether in the market place or outside of it, was her trust in God. It was total. If things worked out well for her, she praised Him. If they did not, she simply tried harder.

But it was not only in God that Tara believed; she believed, in the Devil, too, with the same strong conviction. I had encountered the Devil in Christian scriptures, and remembered when Christ removed many devils from a young girl

102

and allowed them to enter a passing herd of pigs and how these pigs rushed down into the sea and were drowned. I often wondered whose pigs they were and whether the owners were pleased with such a fine miracle. I wondered how the pigs must have felt. I kept these thoughts to myself.

Over the years the friendship between my mother and Tara grew. Tara provided my mother with good quality vegetables at a price that satisfied both ladies, and my mother, in return, allowed Tara to carry over her debts to the following month when things were tight with her. But more important, there was a magnanimity of spirit between them both. One day Tara came to believe that the elder of her two daughters, Savitri, was under the influence, if not of the Devil himself, certainly of one of his more skilful agents. She came to my mother and expressed her fears. My mother, like all good Hindus, knew that the Devil would, from time to time, come in different disguises and 'entice' us. The 'enticement' on this occasion was a young man who, alas, was not of the same high Brahmin caste as Tara.

It was clear to Tara that the devil had a hand in it somewhere; it was, in her words, 'unnatural'. In Pasea village we were all familiar with the Devil and took certain precautions against him. For example, when milk or food was carried from one home to another, who knew what evil spirit it might encounter en route to its destination? To prevent the milk going sour or the food going bad we always placed a bit of lighted coal on the food tray or on one of the containers. It always worked. I came to the conclusion that coal had magical properties.

There were different procedures to ward off evil spirits from a person. Tara told my mother that she was going to take her daughter to the pundit to be *jharayed*.

When you did not know the strength of the enemy, people like Tara and my mother believed that you had to mobilise all your resources. They would have happily prayed to both Rama and Christ, as well as *jharaying* the patient if they felt circumstances demanded a triple force.

Tara was miserable. 'It's my fault. I should have kept a

closer eye on her. I left her too much on her own. I should have found time to speak to her every evening. Now she is working in Port of Spain. How can I see all the way there?'

'How much can one person do?' my mother consoled. 'How can you be in the market and in the home at the same time?' She paused for a while. 'Times are changing, Tara. You think you and I could have gone against our parents' wishes?' They were thoughtful and perhaps sad. Had they got the worst of both times: parents who could not be defied and now children who defied them?

After Tara had gone, my mother said to Daya, 'You make children today, but you don't make their minds.'

'That's true, *Didi*,' Daya said regretfully. My mother finished her lunch and returned to the shop. When I came to the kitchen, Daya looked at me. 'You see how much trouble Savitri giving her mother?' I nodded. 'Well, you musn't do' that. You hear me?' Again I nodded and after a little while said, just to prove that I was immune to such human susceptibilities: 'I don't like boys.' But Daya said nothing. It was as if I had not spoken.

Savitri was taken to the pundit and *jharayed*. A few days later Tara told my mother that she was going to *jharay* her daughter herself. She had her own way of *jharaying*. First she prepared herself by bathing and by praying at dawn, facing the rising sun, as if to absorb some of its energy for the task ahead. If the patient was very ill and lying down, she would take three freshly picked, clean, dry stems of coconut leaves and, saying special Sanskrit prayers, she would move the stems slowly from the head to the forehead, eyebrows, eyes, nose, lips, chin and neck, and in this fashion down to the tips of the toes, after which, the stems were shaken out lest the evil spirit had clung on to them. This was done at least three times. All the while, the resounding Sanskrit words were said over the patient. I saw Tara *jharay* young babies who were making their parent's life a hell by perpetually crying, or by not eating. It was often the case that these babies had been taken to doctors who, with all their London qualifications, could find nothing wrong

104

with them. We felt that if a medical doctor could not diagnose an illness, it was because the cause was outside their training and understanding. There were many who claimed that *jharaying* had helped their babies. Although I could not understand Sanskrit, I judged from Tara's tone of voice that while she was *jharaying* a patient, she was gently coaxing the unkind spirits to leave her patient rather than attempting to expel them forcefully.

I am happy to say that *jharaying* helped Savitri, for soon after, the young man made an appointment to see her parents to discuss his plans with them. He was courteous and said that though he wished to marry Savitri he would not do so without her parent's consent. There and then he invited Tara and Savitri's father to meet his parents. This was unconventional; it was the custom that the girl's parents approach the boy's with great courtesy, and request the favour of an audience with them. This difference in approach, therefore, may have been a result of the difference in caste.

Suffice it to say that Tara and her husband were bowled over by the courtesy, reasonableness and homely charm of this young man's family. My mother was pleased, indeed relieved by their findings, but not so my uncle who was making one of his calls and showing a keen interest in what Tara was telling my parents. When she was finished, my uncle spoke first:

'Look you can't trust these people. Alright, they putting their good foot out in front, that is to be expected. They not stupid and we musn't act as though we stupid either. The situation is simple: they want your good good daughter, Savitri, so they busy putting out honey to catch this fine Brahmin girl. Now you must be cautious. Invite them. I have nothing against that but keep a watchful eye. You don't know them, you don't know when they will spring something on you. Bamb! – and he clapped both hands loudly and made me jump – before you know it, you caught in a trap wriggling to get out.' And with wormlike motions he shook his right hand in an agitated rhythm of agony. My mother said nothing.

My father said, 'We cannot judge them before we see them.

I agree with my brother that you must be cautious. If you would like me to make a few quiet enquiries about the family I am happy to do that. It is too early for any of us to meet them. On this, their first visit, you and Savitri's father and your big boy Ramesh should be present. He is a sensible fellow you have there. Keep it small, don't invite anyone; this gives you an opportunity to speak your mind and whatever fears you have, think about them and bring them to the surface, so that when they leave, at least the important things in your mind would be cleared up.'

My mother said, 'You musn't let it look as if you too anxious, Tara. If they think you too keen, they might even feel something wrong with the girl. Be yourself, but hold back a little. The world is like that.'

When they had all gone my father said, 'If when they come, Tara is happy with what she hears and sees, I don't think she should delay things, she should get the wedding moving. We don't know how much pressure the boy is putting on Savitri, how long she can hold out.'

'Bringing up children these days is not easy,' my mother said, 'the bigger they get, the bigger the worry.'

BETEL NUT

Living deep inside the main Pasea road were the very dark Indians with curly hair. They were called Madrassis, for though none of them were born in Madras they were the children and grandchildren of Indians from that state. They chewed *pan* incessantly, and their tongues and lips and spittle reminded me of raw meat overflowing with blood. I was always ill at ease with them because of this strange habit and had often wanted to ask why they were not like us. For to be candid, it was not only their dark skins and deep red mouths that were contrary, but their customs. Take their way of

106

burying their dead. I would stand and watch from the road-side. Though like us they used to rest the coffin on the ground at the edge of the village in a sombre gesture of farewell, I was surprised to see that they beat drums and danced and made merry all the way to the cemetery. I learnt too that when a child was born they wept bitterly.

I pondered this and asked my mother: 'Do they weep because of all the extra work they have to do when a child is born?'

'No,' said my mother, 'it is because life has so many trials and tribulations, so much suffering. They weep in sympathy for this frail human being who is helpless, who cannot feed himself, who needs the care of so many to survive. He is in a weak position. They are sympathising with the human fate.'

'And do they dance because with death the hardships of life are over?'

'I don't really know. I have never asked them. You must ask your father when he comes.'

The next day came and went and the next too. But on the third day my father seemed less busy and more relaxed and I asked him about the *pan* and the dances at funerals and the wailings at birth.

'The rejoicing at funerals is making an assumption – it is giving the dead man the benefit of the doubt – which is that he has lived a good life and will be moving on to something better.'

I assumed my father meant heaven and said nothing. He continued: 'The wailings at birth also have the same unsenti-mental logic. Life is seldom a bed of roses and for some people their misery is unbearable. Who knows what faces a child? What circumstances await him? So they offer him their sympathy in advance.'

'Should we do the same as the Madrassis?'

'There is nothing wrong with their reasoning, but remem-ber, you belong to an orthodox Sanatanist community and you would constantly have to explain yourself. It may be easier and perhaps wiser to bear it in mind simply as another legitimate position on matters of birth and death.'

And with that my father rose and left. He had forgotten to tell me about the *pan*. My mother said: 'Why don't you ask Ramswammy, he is always chewing *pan*.' I was silent. She continued, 'I hear people say it is good for the gums – makes them healthy.'

'For the teeth too?' I enquired.

'I am talking to you about gums, you are asking me about teeth. Ask Ramswammy. I hear it is like a mild drug.'

'Why would they want to take a mild drug all day?' I questioned.

'When life is painful. Who knows? I don't know the answer. I have had to bear pain without *pan*,' my mother said. 'And it is not easy. If there is something that relieves pain, it must be a help.'

MAHADAYA IS CHOSEN

My mother believed in quality. 'What is the quality like?' she would ask, again and again. It didn't matter what she was purchasing – a pumpkin, a piece of fabric or Indian sweets – the question was the same. I couldn't help thinking that she meshed several things together; wrapped them in fine muslin and called her bouquet, quality. Quality to her meant integrity and worth as well as goodness and value; for she spoke of the quality of flour, rice, a jeweller's craft, a meal, fabrics and people in the same breath.

Testing the quality of some things presented no difficulty to her. Take a pumpkin. The very thinness of its skin, with its natural abstract pattern, said something to her. And it was only after she had tapped a pumpkin twice, listened attentively each time for an answer, and weighed it with her hands, that she would decide to buy it. The methods she devised for testing the quality of other things were just as searching.

108

She purchased all the material for my father's suits and trousers and arranged for the tailor to measure him. (Left to himself, my father never felt the need for new clothes, as long as the old ones continued to fit him.) When she went to the men's clothing shop she would first listen to what the sales clerk had to say about the material she favoured for its feel, colour and texture. She explained to me that material with a certain percentage of wool kept the seams well and stood up to careless and hard wear – and confided that my father was not particular about how he sat or where he sat. If at the end of the clerk's sales talk she was still doubtful, she took out a box of matches and the cover lid of a small tin (all brought for this purpose) and asked for a small sample of the material. This she placed in the lid and there, on the counter, before the clerk's eyes, she would set the sample alight. If it burned rapidly and smoothly she would shake her head and say, 'Just as I sus- pected.' But if she had difficulty setting it alight, and the flame sputtered and went out, or smoked very slowly (like a fine cigar at rest), she would look at the partially-burnt dishevelled piece of material and say, 'Mmmmmm what a yard did you say this was?' Or, 'It is good but I think a bit too heavy. Don't you have a mix with a fine quality wool?'

There was a widely shared belief that small peasant farmers watered the milk they sold, so milk was another product my mother tested. I would be surprised if our supplier, Baboo, watered our milk, because my mother was one of his special customers: she purchased three one-and-a-half-pint bottles every morning and three bottles every evening; and she paid promptly. Even so, in the absence of a laboratory or a govern- ment inspector, she carefully tested her milk for quality and cream content as best she could. If Baboo's fresh milk flowed out without leaving fine globules of fat clinging to the glass, or if it left the bottle with the same flow as water, she concluded that the milk was either tampered with or the cows were poorly fed. If she had any doubts she would perform this experiment before Baboo himself and explain to him what she was looking for and why. To my surprise he never disputed her methods. Again, if after boiling the milk (we had no refrigerator) there was not a substantial thick, yellowish cream at the top, she would ask him why this was so and expect a substantial improvement by the next delivery.

This was the mother I was familiar with, so competent and confident in her dealings with others. But one day there was a glimpse of a person and a time I did not know.

My mother had just finished serving her two grandsons, Anil and Ashok and granddaughter, Indira, their evening meal. The sun had already left the sky and it was cool on the porch. It was the time when the day's work was done and being Sunday it was the time for storytelling, talking about the old days and ironing. I had begun to iron.

There was a closeness between grandmother and grand-children. It was she who had brought them up during much of their primary school years, for there had been no good school where my sister lived and to my mother, having a poor education, was like having an illness – you could get over it with care, but certainly something to avoid if you could possibly do so.

Now in the quiet of the day, they were talking to her about their teachers and laughing their heads off, enjoying their own jokes. Then there came a pause in the conversation when Indira said: 'Nanee, you tell us something now. Tell us about the olden days, about how you came to live here.'

'The golden days she means, Nanee,' grinned Anil, the older of the two boys who was a bit of a show off.

'Life was hard,' she said; 'Don't let anybody fool you about that.'

'Tell us about how you met Nana,' said Indira.

'In those days you didn't meet people. Where would you meet? Weddings were all arranged. We went nowhere, you saw no-one.'

'Didn't you even go to weddings and *kathas?*' asked her granddaughter.

'We were brought up in a different way, you wouldn't understand.'

110

'Well tell us.'

She pulled her fine voile orhni closer, adjusted herself and looked straight ahead past the railway line through the savannah and beyond. Her eyes and forehead drew closer.

'It was your great grandfather who chose me, I don't know why. My eldest sister was already married, to a jeweller, a good one. Three of us were left. I was the youngest. They were all very pretty. I have very small eyes – I can't help it; and my nose bridge is not high, what to do? So when your great grandfather came down to see us and chose me for his eldest son, my parents were a little surprised. To tell you the truth, I was too. My sisters didn't say anything because, though this was a good Brahmin family, compared to us, they were poor. My father who is a straightforward, plain-speaking man, told your great grandfather, there and then, that I had a stammer, and that he might wish to choose one of my sisters instead.

'"It doesn't matter," your great grandfather said. My father was just making sure that later on they wouldn't say they got what they hadn't bargained for; besides I was the youngest and could wait a while. He just wanted them to know beforehand. That was his way.

'"Mahadaya has never done field work," my father also warned. "She will manage a house but I do not think she will fare well in the fields."

'And again your great grandfather said, "It doesn't matter."'

There was a long pause before she picked up the threads again. I continued my ironing.

'I did not know. Three days after my wedding I still did not know. No one said anything to me. No-one even pointed him out to me.'

Indira interrupted, 'Know what, Nanee?'

'Three days after my wedding I did not know who I married.' For a moment there was a silence of incomprehension.

'Didn't you see Nana during the ceremony?' asked her granddaughter gently.

'I was properly covered with my sari and on top of that there were soft lace veils. Your Nana was wearing his wedding crown with all the tassels of flowers and glitter falling and covering his face. What can you see? Besides, we were brought up not to look people in the face, men especially. It was considered common, ordinary, not in good taste to do that. That kind of boldness we did not have. If you got out of line, your family was blamed. It was the character of your mother and the way she brought you up that was then brought into question. So, you kept in line. It was safer that way. What could you do? Besides your parents' parting words were not how much they loved you or cared for you or that if you were ill-treated you should return home. No! No! No! Nothing! Nothing like that!'

'What did they say?' asked Ashok, the younger of the two boys.

'Don't bring shame on your mother and father. Keep up the good name of your family. Remember your other sisters. Their marriage prospects depend on you. One hasty word, one thoughtless act can ruin their chances. Think calmly, no matter what the provocation is, stay calm.'

'What is shame?' asked Ashok. I was somewhat taken aback by this question and could see that it would be ignored. What pictures were going through my mother's mind I cannot say. Outwardly there was an uneasy silence. It was as if the film was still running, but somehow the sounds and images were lost to us. Then Indira spoke.

'So Nanee, how long was it after the wedding before you knew it was Nana you married?'

'One day, I saw two young men standing in the pebbled yard. I didn't know which one it was. Already the third day had passed. I felt the time had come for me to ask but I was not sure. You had to be careful with a thing like that. You did not wish to appear keen – modern; you knew that how you asked, the tone of your voice in the asking, would be repeated, heightened in the telling and retelling in your absence, by the person you asked. I was only fourteen. Your aunty Sumintra was near by and I came up to her and spoke cautiously. "Which one did I marry?"

"Ram."

"I know. But which one is Ram?"

"The tall one. It is easy to tell. He is older than the others."
Then she pulled her grass knife from the smoky rafters of the
kitchen, just as a man would, and left for the plot of land she
and her two brothers farmed.'

'One month passed and I learnt a lot about myself. So too
had everyone else. Everybody knew I could not fetch water on
my head. How the others managed to walk uphill with a large
full oil-tin I did not know. They must have started young, I
thought. I tried several times, but there was always more water
splashed on the road and on me than was in the tin when I
reached home. And there was another thing – I could not cut
grass fast or carry a fat bundle on my head. By the time I had
finished cutting enough for one medium size bundle, Sumintra
had already cut three sizable ones that stood there as judge-
ments against me.

'I tried very hard but my best was not good.

'My father owned a grocery shop and though before I got
married I used to think that shop work was hard, working in
the fields was far worse. There were nettles and prickles and
sharp cutting leaves everywhere and my hands became sore
and red with the grass knife and the sun was without mercy.
It was work for horses not for people.'

'Did you say *that* Nanee?' questioned Anil, much amused
by the phrase.

'All of you think it is one big joke, one big story. But you try
cutting grass in the midday sun.'

'So what happened?' he asked again.

'In the end my mother-in-law decided that I should stay at
home and do the house work instead. Sumintra thought I was
being given the soft work, and that this had been my plan all
along. But though she grumbled, my mother-in-law – to my
surprise – did not budge. Later I put two and two together and
realised that my father-in-law had something to do with this
decision.

'From then on I was left to do the cooking and the cleaning
and the washing. It was a lot to do despite what Sumintra said.

There were nine of us. In my father's house there were only six, and we had a servant who helped with the washing and the cleaning. My mother did the cooking. And yet another thing: no pipes – none – not even in the yard. Imagine trying to wash for nine without any piped water. I had to take everything to the river. If it was sunny, I could dry every thing on the river bank – dry clothes are much lighter to carry. While they dried, I bathed in the cool water and looked around for fruit.

'The people of St. John were helpful. They knew that I could not carry heavy loads.' She paused for a while, 'Perhaps Sumintra told them. I don't know. Some of the men were too ready to help and so I had to be careful as there were times I was alone by the river. I kept a respectable distance for my own sake and my husband's sake and my own family's sake. I was afraid everyone knew my routine and I was alone all day. For the first time I could understand how easy it is to lose one's good name. When you are young and innocent and full of good will towards everybody, you are not prepared for the ways of men; especially if no-one where you live ever offers you a kind word.'

'Everyone in your grandfather's home worked hard. They saved everything and sold almost all their milk, keeping only a little for my father-in-law. They made coconut oil from the copra of their trees. In fact that is how it started with your great uncle Mitra. He used to pick the coconuts.'

'I didn't know we had a great uncle called Mitra,' Ashok said.

'No one talks about him now. He was only ten at the time, about your age, Anil. You look a little like him.'

Anil lifted his eyebrows and looked at himself in the wall mirror. She paused again and wiped her eyes with her orhni. 'He was a gentle boy; quiet and thoughtful...' and again she paused saying something inaudible while she covered her head with her orhni, looking downwards.

'He was way up, high up on the tree. There were a lot of dry coconuts and we needed to make the oil. It was a high curving

114

tree; I used to think it wanted to touch the clouds. The wind was drunk that day. How he must have clung on for his life with his thin hands. Can you imagine the fear? Clinging on and slip-slipping; holding and slipping; trying to hold... he would have struggled... Can you imagine the fear? Knowing, knowing.... he, he ....' She could say no more and I wanted her to stop.

'It was I who found him. He was catapulted away. I could I see his leg. It was unnatural. The way it bent was wrong. I could see something terrible had happened. I lifted him up in my arms; he was as light as a fallen bird. How much did he eat? What could he eat? There was never enough. Cheese, butter, eggs, meat: they were scarce. He didn't have anything to fall back on.

'There was no anaesthetic in those days. Well, not for poor people. They gave him a lot of rum to make him drunk. Your grandfather was there; it took many to hold him down on the table. He became wild the minute they started to cut off his leg. He kept bawling out, "Bhap! Help me! Help me! Bhap! They are killing me Bhap! Stop them! Bhap! Help me, Bhap!"

'What could his father do? What could we do? The doctor said it had to be done. We believed. We did not know any better. We did not know how to speak to a doctor. We did not know you could disagree with a doctor. We did not wish to anger anyone; we were in their hands. Maybe we should have had a second opinion. We didn't know about second opinion in those days. We were poor people. You do not know what it is to be poor.' She paused again and looked at us. 'You should all be working hard at school, be conscientious, and pray that you never become poor. It is hell. It is a living hell I tell you.'

Again she was silent and we waited for her.

'They took him to the hospital in the cart. Bhap carried him into the hospital as if he were a baby. I don't know if the doctor who examined him was good or not. We had no way of knowing. Maybe if I had nursed him... the leg may have knitted up again... Who knows? He died a week after the operation. He knew he was going to die. His eyes grew dull.

He was such a quiet shy boy, not more than ten. He used to call me *didi,* big sister, not *bhowjee,* sister-in-law, as the others.

'For weeks after I kept seeing him; and several times I dished out his food. I felt his spirit was close by. Who knows? You might be Mitra come back to us, Anil?' And she smiled at her grandson.

'If that is so I will avoid climbing coconut trees.'

'To die for a few coconuts; that is what being poor means.'

My mother's words hurled themselves upon me like a mighty wave and their impact stayed with me. To die for a few coconuts that is what poverty means: a denial, a smothering of all the possibilities of a growing life, all for a few coconuts on a tree.

She began moving briskly about in the kitchen. Her tale had ended. The children knew it was time to leave.

'Take this to your mother,' she said, handing Anil a large, well-filled paper bag.

'What's in it?' he asked.

'Just what you had for dinner, it would save your mother cooking dinner for herself and your father.'

After they left I realised that part of Indira's question had not been answered so I said: 'How did you come to be here in Pasea, in Tunapuna? What made you and Pa leave St. John?'

'God knows. But I will tell you what brought it about earlier than anyone could have expected.

'I was big with your eldest brother, and after cooking and washing and cleaning and looking after Maya – I had only just managed to put her to sleep – I sat down in the hammock to take a little rest. I was so tired. I must have dozed off for I did not hear Sumintra arrive. She often came quietly to "catch" me off guard. How long she'd been standing there trying to waken me I do not know.

'"I want my food," I heard her say, shaking the hammock. I jumped. For a moment I didn't know where I was, but the hammock and the rafters and the *chulha* helped me. Then I gathered myself and said:

"It's all there. Help yourself."

116

"I want *you* to give me my food," she repeated.

"I am very tired," I told her. "Help yourself. It is all there."

"I know it is there. Dish out my food." She began to raise her voice, knowing there were no witnesses.

"I am too tired. Why can't you help yourself?"

"Are you going to give me my food or not?"

"Help yourself, Sumintra. I am so tired."

"I will," she said, and with a sweeping movement of her grass knife she cut the support of my hammock. As swift as a bird in flight it happened. I was flat on my back on the ground.

'As God would have it, your father came back early from his weekly journey into Port-of-Spain to buy goods for the shop. At that very moment he entered the yard and saw that lightning sweep of her knife. There and then he must have decided. Not long after we both moved out with Maya – she was two. My mother-in-law tried everything to persuade him to stay – after all, he was the eldest and would become the head of the family when his father died. He might have been thinking about it before, God only knows. I can't say, but in less than three weeks we were here.'

'But you get along very well with aunty Sumintra,' I said. In fact my mother's relationships with all her sisters-in-law were such that you would never think that there had ever been the slightest unkind feelings between them.

'Sumintra was young and headstrong then, she must have been very tired and hungry and frustrated. We were all poor then; but whenever I went home to my own mother, I had lots of fine things – good food, good clothes and a good rest. She had nowhere to go. Besides,' continued my mother, 'when people come to my home it is my duty to treat them well. I was brought up that way. Anyhow that's an old story; think nothing of it. We're all older and wiser.'

I was about ten at the time and Baboo about five times my age; I thought he was very old indeed. He had a white beard and was tall and slim. Before this scandal (you would have thought he would have known better) he could have been Moses or some other prophet. Baboo was a great reader of the holy *Ramayana,* and on this and the *Mahabarata* he had become a village authority.

At first my mother said it was his wife's fault but a day later she said, 'These things happen,' in a sad, resigned way.

It was not in my nature to endure an injustice quietly. I was furious! I expected grown-ups to practice what they preached. Had I ever escaped being beaten for a misdemeanour? There was the time when I'd plopped a dirty mop on my younger sister's freshly-washed long silky hair. One moment she was preening her hair in the sun like a peacock and the next she looked like a wet hen splashed by a passing motorcar on our muddy roads. I felt she deserved it for persistently teasing me about a silly boy in my class. She'd started to howl and ran to my mother. Well, I was thoroughly spanked for that, unfairly I thought; for my mother failed to take into account the provocation. Such injustices I have borne, but never silently.

But Baboo did not practise what he preached. I remembered how, when he ran a small Hindi class at his home, he'd been so particular about pronunciation and with getting the letters of the alphabet written absolutely correctly. He was a real perfectionist.

His wife was a *work house* and looked it. She laboured all day and most of the night. She tended their vegetable garden with its tomatoes, melongene, peas, beans, ochroes and *karaili*. She tended four milking cows, two goats and a few rice plots – enough to make them self-sufficient for the whole year with a little to spare. But alas! they had no children.

Baboo lived in a thatched earth house with two women – his wife and his wife's mother. The latter was a gentle soul, always so pleased to meet anyone. She had a way of putting her hands all round your head and shoulders and would insist that you eat something or take something with you: a mango, sugarcake, or my favourite, a bowl of *pehnoose*. I called it 'the food of the gods' and this made her face light up in a soft wrinkled smile. She told me that one of her neighbour's cows was about to calf and that she would get me some more *pehnoose* in a few weeks. I was delighted with this news, but knowing my mother would say that I should have declined and that I was becoming uncontrollably greedy, I told her that the bowl she'd given me was more than enough and that I would wait until her own cows calved again. She would open the door and tell me to beware of the motor cars and it was only when turning round and waving back to her, that I would be reminded by the careful way she re-entered the house that she was blind.

But a change occurred in this household and with it disaster struck. Baboo's wife had her hands full, but whose idea it was to get house-help for her I cannot say. Whose idea it was that this house-help should be a young woman who slept in, I also cannot say. Whether his wife ever suspected anything I do not know; all I can say is that whenever my mother sent me there for fresh vegetables, this house-help treated me with courtesy and smiles. And she looked quite normal, at least in the daytime when I saw her – nothing like Delilah in a film I had seen. Perhaps she was a firefly at nights?

One Sunday, Baboo's wife came hurrying to see my mother. She was very well dressed and looked so clean and bright that I was quite taken aback. The time of her visit was also unusual. It was not the cool of the late afternoon when a stroll is refreshingly pleasant. It was at two p.m. when the tropical midday sun is an open furnace. Both ladies spoke at length; my mother did a great deal of listening and questioning. When Baboo's wife left I knew that some heavy darkness had struck her.

I knew all this because my mother had a certain way of looking whenever she received distressing news, especially if it was something she could do nothing about.

It was not until the following Monday morning, when my mother was explaining to Daya that our milk would no longer be brought by Baboo, that I began to guess at the tragedy. However, its full nature was only made known to me when Daya told Renee. Renee was sitting on the kitchen doorstep in the comforting morning sun, drinking tea and smoking a cigarette before getting up to 'rub' the clothes. 'Listen here, you mean Baboo the milkman?' asked Renee.

'He took all the money and jewellery with him. They gone to Tobago,' replied Daya from the kitchen, as she busied herself with turning the pots and 'picking' the rice.

'You would think that after a certain age men would settle down? Eh! eh! You know, Daya, if you did ask me to guess who ran off with a young girl this morning, I would never come up with Baboo. Never! Not in a hundred years, man.'

'Me too.'

'It just shows you eh, you never can tell what's going on in people's mind. It's a shut book.'

'Too true. You can't tell from the outside. The outside is the mango skin.'

'So what go happen to the wife now?' asked Renee.

'Well she has the land and the cows; she and the old lady wouldn't starve.'

'How much money so, he gone away with?'

'Must be couple hundreds, good; you know how it is, you don't check every time you put something aside in your own house.'

'So at this age he looking for the sweet life, eh Daya?'

'It look so. But how long it go stay sweet? Sweet life doesn't come free.'

'You telling me. I know that only too well. Look them two children I got. Where their father? Life hard, man, life hard too bad. I was too young and foolish, Daya. I didn't know what life was about.' And with that Renee made a great effort to lift herself and walk towards the tub.

Time passed. It may have been three months, it may have been four, but the worst was yet to come. I heard that Baboo's wife was willing to forgive him and this female firefly, and have them both back and their baby too. I was very cross. I had

120

thought that women were meant to be angry, that they were meant to behave in such a way that men would think twice about leaving the home. This was their only protection. 'Well!' I thought, 'how easy she's making it for him. This attitude simply encourages such irresponsible ways; with such an attitude I marvel that more men don't up and leave their homes.' And there and then I decided that when Baboo returned to the village I would not say 'Good morning' to him; it was the only weapon I had. Hadn't he reprimanded us all in class when we did not get the Hindi alphabet correct? While, while all this time.... I could not put it into words and my throat burned in frustration and anger.

I never did say 'Good morning' to Baboo. I was never given the opportunity. He came and went unannounced when most of the villagers were out in the fields. But he never returned to the village like the prodigal son, despite the magnanimity of his wife and mother-in-law. I saw my father speaking to him once and he did not seem as displeased to see Baboo as I thought he should.

Baboo stayed in the small island of Tobago. His wife was ready to have him back but it was he who couldn't face the village. It was his own ethical standards, his own values he had stepped on. He was strict with us young people and now found he could not be anything but equally severe with himself.

As the years went by, I sometimes thought of him: living on a small, thinly populated island with his son, growing greyer amongst strangers, outside his own East Indian village community. What would the few black fishermen there know of him? What could he tell them? In my mind's eye I used to see him walking on the seashore, a lonely man, with a son who would not understand his father's melancholy.

And the young woman, what became of her? Where would she find that uniquely comforting friendship of the village women with its string of reassuring maternal and sisterly advice, its warmth of shared experiences, that therapy of female understanding and care?

As I grew older, the keenness of my anger left me. When-

121

ever I heard snippets of news about Baboo from Daya I would ask myself: 'Was it worthwhile?' There was no one I could turn to for an answer, but the questions persisted.

'Men are like gods,' I reasoned. 'They can bridle so many things; even the roaring thunderous water that falls from great heights, becoming a fine mist miles away from the fall, can be harnessed; why then can't he harness himself?' As I matured, there were different questions. Was it Youth and Beauty, two divine strengths that are loaned, was it these that Baboo saw slipping hopelessly away from him, that stirred a deep uncontrollable desire to be embraced by both? Was it because he knew he was enjoying the last warm glows of late autumn and thought to delay the coming of winter by the arrival of a son? My wrath subsided and I was confused but still sorry for his wife and her mother.

And so it was, with the passing of still more years, I tried to accommodate all the conflicting emotions and reasoning that played before me. I had an image of Baboo as a man in a canoe, moving speedily with the current towards a mighty waterfall. As he glides along he sees the inevitable before him and then, as if some ancient god of nature was reading his thoughts, an overhanging branch in full blossom, sturdy and strong, appears in front of him, spanning almost half the width of the stream. At the spur of the moment he stands, stretches himself, and seizes the branch while his canoe moves perilously on. He is full of joy, overcome by his good luck as he sits on the branch with the swift current beneath him, feeling safe, secure and excited by this chance thing.

After a while, as the cool air beneath reaches him, he turns about and finds he has the heavens above, the rapids beneath, and a cold damp mist around. It only gradually dawns upon him that he is marooned: his limbs lack the strength of his youth; he cannot make the hazardous journey back to the strong, supportive trunk which is planted firmly in the steady earth, but which is now too too far away from this overhanging branch.

This image of Baboo remained with me.

There was no high altar, no cloistered barricade of highly polished wood between our pundit and ourselves. During a *puja* we were physically and emotionally close to what our pundit was saying, and during the ceremony itself, we had only to wait for a natural pause to whisper to him any concern we might have about the puja.

Religious ceremonies were held at home. Before anything else you had to decide what kind of a ceremony you wanted, whether it was to be a *katha,* a *puja* or a *Ramayana:* a substantial gathering or a homely one. You could take part in the ceremony alone with the pundit, or 'sit' around the *vedi* with your husband or your children or any member of your extended family. Depending on means and preferences, you could invite your close neighbours and friends or the entire village community.

My mother, when she was young and had lots of energy, would invite all our neighbours, as well as anyone who was around my father's rum shop and any of the wandering poor who slept in the open at nights. I have seen her stop men, ragged and foul smelling, as they walked slowly past our shop, and invite them in to have some *katha* food.

It was food which was blessed by God; small portions of it were offered by the pundit to the sacred fire. I used to think that as the sweet smoke lifted up the aroma of gently-burning, freshly-cut pinewood, ghee, camphor and spiced vegetables, the gods were comforted and this made them well disposed to the family making the offering.

Food that has been blessed by God should not be refused by man. Everyone knew this, so when my mother invited the wandering poor and the stationary poor, they knew they were obliged to accept the invitation. To refuse was to court the disapproval of the gods; and so the poor could warm their stomachs with good wholesome food and please both God and their hostess at the same time. After they had eaten and washed their hands she would offer some a length of white cotton suitable for a dhoti and others a silver coin. As they left they thanked God and blessed her.

As the years passed by, she had smaller *kathas* and *pujas*. I preferred those in which a *jhandi* was erected on a freshly cut bamboo pole. These fine flags were of different colours. Whether the gods had favourite colours I did not know, but Hanuman, the god of strength, was represented by red; Ganesh, the god associated with learning and education by yellow; Lakshmi, the goddess of light and wealth, by pink; and the god Shiva by blue.

As human needs vary, it was not unusual to see clumps of bamboo poles in the yards on which there were red, yellow, white and blue flags. They were pretty to look at and gave our red-earth road a feeling of merriment as the brightly coloured flags flap-flapped in the wind.

If you wanted to have a puja in your home, you had first to discuss the matter with the pundit. A day suitable to the family, to the pundit and the gods was chosen. Some days were very good days for starting a business or moving into a new house or getting married. You didn't have to worry about choosing your day, the pundit always knew which day was auspicious.

After the date was settled, you had to contact a *sadhu* or a pundit's helper. Our *sadhu* was called Sadhu by everyone in the village, grown-ups and children alike: I do not think anyone knew his name. During the service our *sadhu* and our pundit only had to look at each other and each knew what the other wanted. About a week before the puja, my mother went over the list of essential ingredients with Sadhu. After a time she became quite an expert and only discussed her difficulties with him.

'Sadhu, I can't find any *supari;* I tried everywhere.'

'You tried Ramlogan's place?'

'Everywhere. The market, Green Street, Baboo.'

'Not to worry. I have some.'

'I can depend on you?'

'Yes. When I come to build the *vedi,* I'll bring it.'

'Don't let me down now; I'm not going to look any more.'

Sadhu would nod his head and after a respectful pause take his leave.

I delighted in the fragrance exuded by freshly cut pine and I could not have enough of it. For me a puja was, as well as being a spiritual occasion, a time of high sensory excitement. The pundit would gather together from the *tharia* sweet grated coconut, ripened sultanas, uncooked unpolished rice and home-made ghee and place them gently on a pyre of freshly-cut glowing pinewood with its camphor ablaze. The sweet aromatic smoke would embrace the entire house and the surrounding yard and wrap up everyone with a feeling of warmth, of significance and peace of mind.

There is something serene about a home and its surroundings when they are orderly and bright with cleanliness and sunlight; when, wherever you look, the drains, the yard, the floors are all fresh and pleasing to the eye; one could not but be comforted. The whiter-than-white *dhoti* and *phagree* of the pundit; his richly embroidered *kurta* in golden yellow satin and his long flowing elegant *angochar* of fine material and dancing tassels, would all help to make a religious ceremony, held at our home, a very special celebration.

The rich penetrating perfume of tropical marigolds, small old-fashioned highly scented purple-red roses and the temple flowers had the same effect as heady wine. These intoxicating scents were often mingled with a ruby-coloured, warm perfume that the *sadhu* sprinkled on the faithful as the service came to an end. I liked being sprinkled with perfume from above, and we children could point to the exact spots where the sprays fell upon us.

It was not only by the perfumed air that you could tell the *katha* was coming to an end, but also by the sounds and buzz of activity coming from the kitchen. One of the *sadhus* would blow the large conch shell and the pundit would ring a small brass bell; then another *sadhu* would strike the small gong while the pundit would call upon the gods in Sanskrit, individually and in a prescribed order and ask for their blessings. Finally he hails – *ki jai* – each one by name. All present stand up, except sleeping children, and join the pundit in greeting the gods. Then a *sadhu* takes the *arati* from the pundit and brings it to all present. What a comforting gesture!

The *arati* is a flickering light hovering around a piece of burning camphor placed in a large glistening brass *tharia*. The camphor is lit by the priest and first presented to the gods by passing it round and round the *vedi*. Then this flickering dancing light, exuding warmth and glowing in all its symbolic meaning, is offered to all. As the *arati* is placed before you by the *sadhu,* who stands holding it with both hands, you also make a symbolic gesture with both your hands. You appear to embrace the fire with your cupped fingers and pass its warmth over your head, forehead, ears, cheek, neck, shoulder and chest in one smooth movement.

But first, you place one cent, one penny or a silver coin in the glowing brass *tharia* which mirrors the moving flame. If you don't have any money, it doesn't matter, you must still embrace the warmth of the radiant light and shower the top half of your body with it. Mothers would take the *arati* for their sleeping babes.

Once I tried to dip into the warm leaping flame twice, but Sadhu very quickly admonished me, not because it was wrong, as he later explained, but, 'If you do it, so will the others and it will take me twice as long to reach everyone.'

After the *arati,* the sharing of *panchamirit* followed, a sweet liquid of milk and honey and ghee and the aromatic magical *Tulsi* leaves. We would take this in the palm of our cupped hands. We would only get one tablespoon. It was never enough! Then would come what we had been waiting for: *prasad,* made by my mother. It came in a large wooden tray; rich and crumbly, made of ghee and butter and sugar and flour and raisins. It was served with freshly grated coconut that had been lightly sweetened with sugar and sultanas. We would each receive a paper bag of this delight. It was hot and smelt good and felt good in our hands. But there was more to come and so we would hang about waiting to be called.

Then from the kitchen came the teasing excitements of spiced, savoury food: *paratha,* pumpkin, *khir,* curried potatoes with *channa, karhi, bhajee, chataigne,* curried mango and boiling hot rice with *kachourie* served separately and the mouth watering pickles – *achar* or *kuchala.* I was not the only one whose thoughts strayed from time to time to the food, for I heard the pundit say to my father: 'I could see the children were getting hungry and restless and I know that *Bhagwan* will understand why I brought the service to a close a few minutes early; nothing essential has been lost.'

Everyone was amused and pleased, especially we children who did not understand much of the ceremony which was conducted in Sanskrit and explained to the gathering in Hindi.

On such days a feeling of good will would emanate from all those present: fifty to a hundred or more busy people who found time to come and listen to the pundit's readings and expositions from the sacred books. A deep-seated inner satisfaction was experienced but rarely spoken of.

At the end of the day my mother would be pleased that her invitations had been accepted, for one never knew how many were coming. Invitations were given by word of mouth and received and accepted in the same way. The fact that so many remembered and came and enjoyed what had been prepared, gave her a feeling of relief as well as contentment.

But there were times when despite her experience and skill some food was left over. Then my mother would fill up many an enamel bowl and send me with them to the homes of those who had promised to attend but did not, with this message: 'Ma says that she prepared for you and as you did not come, she has sent your share.'

If at the end of the day there was still some food left over, the remainder would be taken to a river and placed on its bed so that the fishes too could rejoice.

PART FOUR

FORMS OF IMPERFECTION

DAUGHTERS

In the early 1950s, there were two Catholic schools, run by nuns and priests, which had attained good academic reputations. Their students were coming first in the island in science, mathematics and languages and these achievements were loudly proclaimed by present and former students and their parents.

My father learnt of the opening of Fatima Girls' High School, a new Catholic school, through Father John who from time to time called on him at his hardware shop to discuss what they, if asked, might have called a philosophy of life. My father had a deep yearning to discuss the unexplainable, and Father John provided him with this opportunity. Their discussions were most amiable, invariably ending over a glass or two of brandy.

Father John had explained that Fatima Girls' High School – opening about two miles away in Curepe – was going to be a branch of the prestigious St. Joseph's Convent in Port of Spain, the teachers coming from the same order of nuns. As my elder sister had been a student at the Convent many years ago, my mother promptly made me four St. Joseph's convent uniforms, from fine quality material, with very generous hems.

She asked my father to get her some more application forms to the school and sent me with them to relatives and friends. Of the six forms I distributed, only two bore fruit. This was not because Hindu parents did not believe in higher education for girls. There were other 'invisible' considerations: Hindu girls of marriageable age from privileged homes had always been treated by their parents as if they were made of

131

the finest porcelain and, unfortunately, the secondary schools of a high standing were in the capital and distant from the Indian villages in the wide alluvial belt of sugarcane and rice.

Their own experiences and observations had left Hindu parents distrustful of the warm energy and daring of youth, and the pitfalls of teenage infatuations, particularly in the environment of a city far away from home. They kept these fears to themselves and their daughters at home.

This, however, was not what they said and my uncle (having declined an application form) spoke for most when he said: 'There is no need for a woman to be more educated than her husband. In fact,' he emphasised, 'it is to the benefit of all concerned that she be a little less... Look at it this way, in the long run she gets married and then her Latin and French and Algebra would be of no help. Indeed they might prove to be a hindrance. Why a hindrance? She would acquire airs and a self importance that could be an irritation to all concerned.'

My mother said nothing at first, but having offered her brother-in-law a drink of freshly squeezed orange juice and seeing he was now rested, she returned to the subject. 'All that you have said is true, there is no denying that, but times are changing. Our sons and daughters are different from us. We all hope when the time comes your daughter Parbatee will marry someone good. But there is no guarantee. If, heaven forbid, she should not be blessed in marriage, it would be better for her to leave her husband's home and find a job. That would be preferable to a life of humiliation, cruelty and suffering.'

'That is easier said than done,' my uncle replied hastily, vexed that his elder brother's wife should express the sentiments of a young wayward girl. 'What will become of the children? Perhaps if there's only one child we can all rally round: but two, three, four children, what then?'

'If he's a man with no pride in himself, who prefers to spend his money on amusements and give nothing to his children, it's better not to know such a man.

My mother spoke with strong convictions and my uncle did not know what to make of it. He got up and said wearily,

'It is getting late.' She thanked him for coming and enquired after my aunt and Parbatee's brothers and sister.

FATIMA GIRLS' HIGH SCHOOL

I was one ball of excitement when, in my new squeaking white plimsolls and shop-new socks and Panama hat, I put my left foot on the pedal of my brand-new green ladies bicycle and pushed off with my right, throwing my legs over, as I had observed men do. I was the first female to ride a bicycle in the village and was quite unaware that there was a lady's way of mounting one.

Dangling from the handle was my new, real leather bag. It was a gift from my brother-in-law and it smelt good. He told me: 'You see this bag here, it will last you not a single day less than twenty-five years. Nothing to beat leather when you think of it.' I believed him; he was my brother-in-law.

I was on my way to my new school – Fatima Girls' High School (FGHS). There was joy in having so many new things, a delight in the feel and smell of newness, but my inner excitement was more the result of a feeling I kept to myself. It was so powerful that I hummed and sang my favourite tunes along quiet patches of the journey as I cycled on. Something within me had grown. I felt I was getting taller, that a tight iron cage which had long clasped my brain and chest had gone.

This sensation affected my eyes too. A mist had lifted. Greens were deeper and darker. Dew drops were larger and seemed to laugh as they playfully rolled down leaves and petals. I began to smile at passers-by. I couldn't tell them, but I knew that I would never again be beaten in school. I would no longer have to queue up for pain, no longer hear that SWOP SWOP of a leather belt falling upon me, no longer would I weep, humiliated.

The cycling was beginning to make me warm, but the morning breeze was cool and refreshing.

I pedalled on past Monte Grande, a residential area of small brown jalousied wooden houses and a few single-storey houses of brick and concrete. In front of all of them, no matter how crooked the wooden front steps, there was a flower garden, usually of roses, gru-gru palms, ferns, crotons, begonias, marigolds, dahlias, zinnias and many others whose names no-one knew, for it was common not to know the names of trees and flowers even in one's own garden.

As I approached the Imperial College of Tropical Agriculture, I was struck by the thought that within these buildings people were engaged in scientific research. Apart from knowing it had to do with cocoa, coconuts, sugar and coffee, I had little idea exactly what was entailed, but the term scientific research sounded grand. The spacious, regulated pattern of the buildings and their grand scale made me realise that these ideas had come from a society wealthier than my own.

Separating the main buildings was a green sea of lawn, of varying depths of colour, unruffled and neat. At intervals, there were mature flowering trees. All avenues leading to any part of this complex were lined with neatly trimmed shrubs. There were outhouses and dwelling places, built of substantial materials and painted white, their roofs of green galvanized sheeting. The houses were partly hidden from view (though they were along the road) by clumps of palms, purple poinsettia hedges, tall green shrubs, pink and white oleanders, climbing clematis and red and yellow flamboyant trees. Invariably attached to the closed front gates of these houses was the sign: 'Beware of the Dog.'

But Fatima Girls' High School was a modest building. The two senior classes were upstairs and our class, the more senior, was taught by two nuns: Mother Mary Rose, the principal, and Mother Anthony. Every morning they arrived from St. Joseph in a Morris car driven by a novice.

Mother Mary Rose was a short, plump, white nun. She was usually smiling and spoke simply no matter what the issue.

Mother Anthony, who always stepped back to allow Mother Mary Rose to pass, was slim, 'high coloured' and younger. Her manner suggested strong self-discipline, yet she was alive to the warmth of human contact.

Downstairs was the junior school, taught by middle-aged ladies, good Catholics themselves, who saw it as their duty to help their pupils, in turn, become good Catholics.

In most secondary schools each subject was taught by a specialist teacher. At FGHS every subject in our class was taught by Mother Anthony, every subject except Scripture. It was not that Mother Anthony could not teach us scripture, more perhaps that it was the one subject Mother Mary Rose felt competent to handle in the senior school. In addition she taught something called Religious Instruction. For this a small, pocket-sized book with a blue cover, called a catechism, was used.

As we had no such thing in Hinduism I was intrigued by this neat small book because it asked the most exciting questions imaginable, though I had difficulty with some of the answers. For example: Question (1) – Who made you? Answer – God made me. Few religions would argue with that, although people without religion would. Question (2) Why did God make you? That I thought was a very difficult one. I felt the way of knowing for certain was to ask God. But how would I know He was answering the question and not, say, the Devil? Again, it might be me who was answering and thinking it was God. I had no way of knowing for certain how to get round this problem.

But about one thing I was sure, the answer could not come from people, for I had observed that they seldom gave the real reasons for their own actions. For example a man might behave in a certain way because he was arrogant, greedy or jealous or mean or lazy or just couldn't be bothered; but I had never heard any grown-up, not even once, give any of these as their reasons. I concluded that men were ill-equipped to presume reasons for the actions of a supreme being - the creator of the entire universe.

The answer to that second question in the neat small blue book was: 'God made me to know him, to love him and to serve him in this world and to be happy with him forever in the next.' This answer I thought would also please most religions. But as I flipped through the pages, the questions and answers became more and more foreign to me, and I could see it was a book meant for Catholics.

For almost two years I cycled from Tunapuna to Curepe not only in the mornings and afternoons but also at midday. Then everyone had a substantial hot lunch; Mother Mary Rose and Mother Anthony had theirs brought for them at noon by car in a white enamel food carrier.

Non-Catholics were expected to join in chapel prayers in the morning and the saying of the rosary after lunch. Like the others I purchased a black net headscarf, which fell below the shoulders and was kept in place by two pieces of ribbon tied together under one's hair.

Religious instruction was given to Catholic girls in private by Mother Mary Rose, in preparation for their Confirmation. This meant that at no time was I exposed to concepts such as mortal sin and venial sin and I had never heard our pundit classify sin in this way. During scripture lessons, therefore, I found myself quite at sea with these new religious concepts.

Once, Mother Mary Rose mentioned the word hell and I whispered to Janice, who sat besides me, 'There is no hell.'

'What is that you are saying, Kamla?' Mother Mary Rose asked, stopping the lesson. I stood up.

'Nothing important, Mother Mary Rose.'

'I'll be the judge of that. You have already disturbed the class, so do not waste any more of my time.'

There was silence.

'So you don't believe in hell, isn't that it.'

'Yes, Mother.'

'You are wondering how I knew, aren't you?'

I could hear the nervous shuffling of girls behind me.

Mother Mary Rose under normal conditions looked like a gentle combination of milk and honey, but on this occasion I felt the broad shadow of a hawk's wing circling overhead. I awaited the inevitable.

'Hell is a place where an everlasting fire rages. This fire burns on and on and on. It never dies. It is a place where the pain inflicted is so intense that no pain on earth can be compared with it.'

I concluded it was not a place anyone would wish to enter of their own accord. And to my surprise words such as evil, wicked, the damned, mortal sin – all unpleasing sounds – came gushing out from the milk and honey Mary Rose.

'What happens when they die?' I asked, feeling that so much torture must result in a most welcome death.

'The soul never dies,' said someone behind me.

'Thank you, Agnes,' said Mother Mary Rose, with an all-knowing smile. Now Agnes was not the brightest of girls and so I realised that now I had entered a place unknown to me but familiar to everyone else. This was Catholic territory. I decided to stand still, not knowing where the pitfalls were.

'So hell means eternal pain and suffering to the soul.'

I said this in quiet confirmation, wishing to leave the pit, not knowing which low door would fling open and what terrors I might encounter next.

'Exactly, but of course, God in his infinite wisdom and mercy, and through the grace of our Lord Jesus Christ who died for us all on the cross...' and she paused as she bent down to pick up a piece of fallen white chalk. But before she could continue, Agnes, who normally said nothing in class even when gently encouraged by Mother Anthony, said:

'...Created purgatory so that we may be cleansed and be ready to live with him for ever in the next.'

Mother Mary Rose must have intended to put forward her beliefs with greater elaboration but now her sails were trimmed by this same Agnes. The bell went, but there were important things she had left unsaid, so rising from her chair she declared:

'The fires of purgatory are no less intense than those of hell, but there is a very very important difference: the souls in

137

purgatory are not damned for all eternity, they may be saved even at the latest hour. By our prayers to the blessed Virgin Mary and the saints and by having special masses said, their length of time in purgatory can be substantially reduced.'

It was good to leave the classroom and walk about the playing field in the sun. It was then I learnt from Janice, a good, quiet Catholic girl, about another place: Limbo. I had never come across it before and wondered whether my father or our pundit had.

Kind and considerate Janice, who did so want to help me find my way to the Catholic church, suggested that Limbo might be situated somewhere between heaven and purgatory. A place neither of pain nor joy – a sort of weightless place where the law of gravity did not apply. Whom did God send there, I wondered, and was about to ask, when Janice added 'Babies not baptised in the Catholic church go there.'

So were there Hindu babies, Moslem babies and Presbyterian babies all floating about like angels on Christmas cards; perhaps making gurgles neither of pleasure, nor of pain?

It only then dawned upon me where Mother Mary Rose thought that grown-ups of all other religions went. Her certainty greatly disturbed me.

Our pundit had made me feel that in heaven there were all kinds of people, all faiths. 'Do good,' he would say, 'that's all that matters. Live your life in such a way that every living thing is happier because you have passed that way. If you see a plant drying up, give it water, if a dog is hungry give it food; if a bird is thirsty show it where it can drink.'

These things were said in a quiet, unassuming way and because of this, and in comparison to the convictions of Mother Mary Rose in the infallibility of the doctrines of the Catholic Church, I began to wonder whether there might not be greater worth in what was complex, indiscernible and sophisticated than in a simple message such as: 'Do good unto others.'

School continued in its usual routines, but whenever I was alone, the vivid description of Mother Mary Rose's hell returned to me.

After a while, I began to wonder whether God intended to save my entire family through me. Should I warn my father that salvation lay only in becoming a Catholic?

I spent many hours in the back garden drawing pictures of Limbo, Purgatory and Hell on the earth with a dry stick. I was always completely outside these spheres, looking in at them from over a wall. I drew pictures of our pundit and Mother Mary facing each other: the former always smiling and the latter warning me with her eyes, neck, shoulders and chest.

'Come,' said Mother Mary Rose, rising from my drawing, taking me to an enormous monument in the sky. Inside, the arches clasped their hands overhead and spoke of authority, power and strength. They looked down at me from their great height, these dignified pinnacles of solemn concrete, iron and stone – moving circles of light and air, watching me with an assurance that I marvelled at. The pillars and arches rose higher and still higher, unencumbered by doubt, vaulting upwards, skywards, heavenwards. 'Behold thy God,' she said, and disappeared.

I was miserable and walked slowly from the garden.

I kept to myself. I needed solitude.

A certain kind of reasoning was beginning to gnaw at the roots of all the things I held dear.

I thought about the vast wealth of the Catholic Church. Catholic priests were teaching pure mathematics and physics, subjects recognised as being at the frontiers of a better understanding of our planet. Students at the boys' College of the Immaculate Conception (commonly known as St. Mary's, College) were coming first on the island in science. There was so much organisation, discipline and achievement. All the questions and answers were in one small neat blue book, which one could keep in one's handbag. This was modern urban and sophisticated. The high altar, the confidence, the power: it all seemed closer to an omnipotent being than the simple rural ways of the Hinduism I knew.

Our altars were not high, they were of earth, built at home and made temporarily for the occasion. Was it this Earth we worshipped, its soil and water and the mysterious life therein? Our temples were small: places for individual prayer and devotion, quiet and clean and very modest. There was nothing in our temple anyone would wish to steal. Our old people sat yoga-fashion on the floor, as did the pundit and our offerings were flowers, ghee, milk, water, honey or sugar and rice. Our services were conducted in Sanskrit, which I did not understand, and they were usually small family prayers in the home, though quite often we had community get-togethers when friends and neighbours were invited to listen to the exposition of sections of the sacred works: the *Bhagavad Gita,* the *Vedas,* the *Mahabharata,* or the *Ramayana.*

Because of all these things and because of what Mother Mary Rose had said, my mind was restless. My former concept of God had been shaken. I wondered why God didn't say after sentencing someone to a spell in such a hell, 'Enough is enough,' and release them? Didn't He forgive? Mother Mary Rose was adamant that God would not be 'fooled'. I was sure that a God who could see into the hearts of men would know if someone was truly sorry. 'But how does the Church know when someone was truly sorry?' I asked myself and received no answer.

Were non-Catholics doomed to hell? This was a most disturbing thought. It didn't seem right. After all didn't we Hindus go to the temple and give offerings and pray and fast and give to the poor? Didn't we go to the help of others when called? My mother helped so many. She gave credit to wives and mothers in the shop against her better judgement when their husbands and sons were out of work, knowing she would not be paid. And didn't people come to my father for advice? Didn't he leave his business and travel with them to see the land they were thinking of purchasing? And didn't he advise them as if they were his own brothers or sons? Wouldn't God remember these things?

Despite all this reasoning and despite our pundit's reassurance that there were many paths to the Divine One, I decided to ask my father for his views. I was not sure how to approach the subject and went about it not at all as I had first intended.

One day, after he had his lunch, I began by describing hell to him as vividly as Mother Mary Rose had done and then said that according to the Catholic Church we in the village were heading towards this place. My father listened patiently and then quietly replied: 'When you meet someone can you tell whether he or she is a Hindu or a Christian?'

'Oh yes,' I said, 'I can tell the difference when I meet someone.' My father looked surprised. 'Well then,' he said, 'tell me how you can?'

The question seemed too simple, for surely, I though anyone can tell the difference. 'Christians wear hats, gloves, stockings, high-heeled shoes, have English names, go to dances and eat beef with a knife and fork. Indians wear orhnis, long full skirts and blouses, marry in saris, wear sandals or chappals, and beautiful gold jewellery at weddings, have Hindi names, eat a lot of home-grown fresh vegetables with their fingers.'

I could see that my father was disappointed with my answer but he was calm. 'I was not referring to the unimportant things the eyes see readily,' he said.

'What then?' I asked.

'Is one more honest than the other?'

'I would not be able to tell if one man is more honest than another unless I were to place temptation in their way and see how they respond,' I said smiling, trying to show that I was not always simple minded.

'Similar temptation I presume?' provoked my father.

'If possible the same temptation,' I replied, beginning to be on my guard.

'The men's circumstances at the time of the temptation should be similar?'

'Similar or identical,' I said smiling more broadly, for I, noticed that my father was pleased with my effort to be fair to both men on trial.

'Well, I will tell you,' said my greying father. 'In my long experience both in business and outside it, I have found that the differences in religion have no effect on the way men live their lives and conduct their businesses. Devout Hindus and devout Christians have more in common than they think and the rascals on both sides too. One group is using hell fire to keep us in line and the other is using reincarnation. No one knows. Pure guesswork. Were you to become a Catholic you would be moving from one form of imperfection to another. Your second position would be no improvement on the first. In fact I suspect it may be worse; for Hinduism is more open; therein lies its strength and weakness. We expect to see Catholics in heaven; they are sure we won't be there.'

With these words I was calmed and soothed. My former confidence in Hinduism, in the village and in myself was reinstated. My father's words were a balm, a salve to my inner spirit, as well as an invigorating wine. As he rose to leave, he paused, turned and, seeing my smiling face and its relief, hesitated a little while. It was as if he was not sure whether this was the time to speak his thoughts. Then he spoke: 'When you are older you can decide; you are too young... And don't believe everything those nuns tell you.'

FATIMA: ANOTHER APPARITION

Freed from the fear of hell by my father's agnosticism and from the dogmatic certainties of Catholicism by his close observation of human behaviour, I threw myself into all aspects of school life with vigour and optimism. I was captain of the school's cricket team and an enthusiastic wicket keeper. I was equally good at netball and after practising seriously at home, became the best 'shoot' in class.

Mother Anthony continued to teach us eight subjects. She did her best but competence in eight was too much to ask of anyone, and certainly too much to ask of her, though at no time did she speak of this burden. Unknown to us, her strengths became ours; so did her weaknesses.

As we approached the end of the second year we had not moved from the geometry of parallel lines; areas and circles had yet to be introduced. French was not treated as a living language and soon I devised my own pronunciation, based on the simple principle that words ought to be pronounced as they are spelt – English being the medium I used. One example will suffice. *Je suis* became for me phonetically: 'Gee soois'; in this way I was able to avoid spelling errors in written French. At the time it seemed a sensible measure to use and it worked, for I only wrote French, but the day of reckoning came. Spanish was a different matter altogether. We enjoyed its rhythm, its music and its sound; indeed, we were completing our Senior Cambridge syllabus in less than half the time usually taken.

Meanwhile, however, black clouds were encircling the school but like everyone else I was unaware of them. Whether Mother Anthony could not take our class any further or whether the decision-makers behind this venture did not wish to introduce more senior staff: no one knew. It may have been that the school was not paying its way. No reasons were given. What our parents were told during the Easter holidays of the second year was that the school was closing down at the end of its third term.

Closing down! No more? Gone as if it had never existed? Why? Where would we go in September? Why hadn't they told us it was only a two-year thing? I was miserable. We in the senior class were already too old. I and a few others were thirteen but there were many who were fourteen. Entrance examinations to schools were in the main for the eleven plus.

But there was a silver lining to this cloud for a chosen few. Quite by chance I learnt that arrangements were being made for the brighter girls in our class to be transferred to St. Joseph's Convent in Port of Spain. It was one of the finest girls' schools on the island. I was relieved to learn this. I had entered the classroom during the lunch break and saw Mother Anthony speaking to Magaret De Souza in quiet hushed tones at the back of the class room. 'Is something the matter?' I asked Magaret, as Mother Anthony's footsteps faded.

'The school is making arrangements for a few girls to be transferred to the Convent,' she said.

'That's good,' I smiled.

'Only a few of the bright girls; it's a secret,' she added excitedly. That evening I took this excitement home. My father said, 'You see, hard work does pay.' I had been first in my class since the school began, that is every term except the very first. I was certain that I would be chosen. My mother asked, 'And what is going to happen to the others? A church school should look after everyone. Where will the other children go?' She was particularly disappointed. She had encouraged parents to send their daughters and felt personally responsible. But then my mother always had a way of worrying about other people's children as though they were her own.

During lunch breaks Mother Mary Rose began interviewing girls in my class, as well as the class next in seniority. I gradually became anxious as days passed into weeks. Each fresh day I felt would be my turn. I looked for signs that said, 'Today you will be told what you knew all along.'

My turn finally came.

I was all smiles as I went towards Mother Mary Rose. She smiled too and then said, 'Well, I suppose you had no difficulty making arrangements for yourself.' I couldn't understand what she was saying. Making arrangements for myself? Is that what I was expected to do? My stomach felt empty and I did not answer at first. She continued, 'If you haven't, I will gladly give you a recommendation; I speak for Mother Anthony too, of course.'

'I told my parents about the scheme you have for bright girls going to the Convent.'

'I am so sorry there has been a misunderstanding here. That scheme is for Catholic girls. You may not know, Kamla, but it is a mortal sin for Catholic girls to attend non-Catholic schools.'

'But I have come first four times. Doesn't that count?' I pleaded, in the way that throughout history the weak plead for justice before the strong. I was beginning to lose control of my eyes and lips.

'That's not the issue. As I have just said, Mother Anthony and I would be only too happy to give you a recommendation. How can I give you a place and refuse a Catholic girl one? More is at stake here, much more than merit, Kamla. One's soul. One's immortal soul, Kamla.'

I did not believe in hell but my anger raged and my throat burned with a rising volcanic intensity. At that moment, had I the power, I would have created a hell such as she had once described and gladly put her in. Instead, I went to the wash room and wept bitterly. I wept for my mother and for my father and for myself. I asked, 'Is this fair? Is this just?' But no one answered. 'Oh God!' I cried again, 'Please,' the pain welling up in my throat setting it on fire. 'Why? Tell me why, please.' My mouth quivered. 'I do not understand. I worked hard, you know I worked hard.'

But there was nothing there.

Outside, a wispy transparent cloud moved on effortlessly. I could hear voices from the playing field. Nothing had changed. I washed my face and thought, 'What must I do now? How will I carry this disappointment home to my mother? Maybe I shouldn't have questioned hell and heaven before Mother Mary Rose. Had I kept silent, had I kept my doubts to myself, my situation might have been different. And I came to the conclusion that from now on, no matter how disturbed I was about anything, I would keep it to myself, for there was much to be gained by being silent.

As I cycled home, it gently dawned upon me that my mother might have told some of the customers in the shop that I would be going to the Convent. A part of me withered.

I came home. The shop was busy. I changed into my home things and decided to help my mother, hoping that this would soften the impact of what I had to say.

'I am not a Catholic,' I said, looking at the scales and playing with the weights. 'It is only Catholics they are sending to the Convent.'

My mother said nothing. Her face looked puzzled then very sad. She knew and I knew and Mother Mary Rose knew that there were bright non-Catholic girls at the Convent. 'Did you have a row?' she asked.

'No.'

'Did you say anything about religion to upset them?'

'No.'

'Go and eat. When your father comes we will decide what to do.'

I went out in the garden and hid my shame and embarrassment amongst the shrubs.

MOVING OVER

There were a number of small private schools, but as they could only be described as commercial makeshift operations, I applied to the only secondary school of substance in the area: St. Augustine Girls' High School (SAGHS).

One Saturday morning I cycled to the school, a large, rambling, old wooden building, to take its entrance examination. I was placed in one of its three temporary outhouses and there took examinations in English and Mathematics.

Two weeks later I received a letter with the joyful news that the school was willing to have me. I was so thankful and relieved.

It was a Canadian Presbyterian school. I had first met a Canadian missionary, Mrs. Murray, many years earlier when I was in primary school. She was like a kind old aunt. Every Sunday, at about three o'clock, when the tropical sun is unfriendly and fierce, she left a comfortable cool home, with a well-kept prolific orchard of grapefruits, shaddocks, oranges, limes and mangoes, a garden of orchids and a most amiable husband, and entered alone into the heart of our village, a stronghold of Hinduism and to a lesser extent of Islam. We children welcomed her and rushed to help her with her bags, her missionary burden.

She had got the permission of a well-to-do Hindu to hold her Sunday school under his upstairs house. It was cool and spacious under this house; the pillars were about eight feet tall so we had much head room. Mrs. Murray's two baskets were filled with good tidings. In one of them there were neat stack of the most beautiful, richly-coloured used Christmas cards we had ever seen. There were cards with deep red and yellow satins; cards with bright gold and sparkling silver paper; and cards covered with glistening, sand-papery stardust. Some had dark cherry-red ribbons and the quality of the paper was so exquisite to the touch that I would at times caress it with my cheeks. A few cards opened out into houses, carnations and hanging stockings.

Many of these Christmas cards had been sent to Mrs Murray and her family, but she also gathered cards from Canadian friends and well-wishers. As Sunday school came gradually to a close (having sung hymns and listened to *Bible* stories in much the same way we listened to *Ramayana* and *Mahabarata* stories at home) each of us received one of the gold and silver Christmas cards. At times we fought over them. On one occasion, five-year-old Roopnarine began crying because he had received a card with Jesus just standing. It was quite a plain card and it was clear he wanted it exchanged. I offered him one with a gleaming red steam engine from which over-flowed balloons the colours of the setting sun, ribbons and bright smiling faces. He stopped crying a once. I tried to offer this plain card of a standing Jesus to the next boy, but he shook his head and would not accept it. He pointed to the one he wanted: Jesus performing a miracle in robes of deep purple and golden green. Strong amber, rich ruby-reds, luxurious shades of purple and vermilion hues: that's what we all wanted.

Then we sang, 'Jesus loves me this I know, for the Bible tells me so,' at the top of our voices, though none of us had opened a bible. One day Mrs. Murray brought the ten commandments in her basket. They were just a lot of do's and don'ts. I was disappointed for I had expected grand things, since the word commandment is long and has a weighty sound. Each commandment was written on a thin strip of Bristol board about two inches wide and nine inches long. She called them 'steps'. We were given two long parallel white strips upon which we glued these steps, so building a ladder. The more steps we had on our ladder the better. Of course, you were not allowed to glue on a step if you did not know the commandment on that step by heart.

I found the commandments quite easy to follow. *Honour thy father and thy mother.* We Hindus all did, though we did not have a commandment telling us to do so. *Do not covet your neighbours ox or wife or ass* did not present us with any difficulty either. We did not know the meaning of covet and assumed it meant 'take'. None of us in Sunday school would have wished to take any of these from our neighbours because we had no place to hide them and wouldn't know what to do with them if we had; such a commandment we saw as sound common sense.

I noted there was no commandment which said thou shalt not covet thy neighbour's husband and wondered what could possibly be the reasons for such an omission. It was not the sort of question I felt I could ask Mrs. Murray, for over the years I found grown-ups tended to misinterpret the reasons why a question was asked. Questions asked to satisfy a natural curiosity seemed to them such a waste of time. I kept it to myself.

So, being a student at SAGHS was my second encounter with Canadian Presbyterianism. Compared with Roman Catholicism, I felt that while with the latter, you and your three ox-carts, filled high with heavy boxes and trunks, arrived at the gates of Heaven tired and weary; with the former, you arrived at Heaven's gates with something as light as Mrs. Murray's handbag. You would also be smiling, happy and ready to offer tea and scones to the angels.

Though I was thankful that I had been offered a place I felt apprehensive the first morning I cycled to St. Augustine. I realised that some of the girls might know me for I had frequently cycled past their school, and feared that some would see me as belonging to the 'other' school, a member of the 'other' tribe now seeking shelter with them.

When I arrived I found something comforting about the old timber, brown jalousies and the rambling disrepair of the building. There was no arrogance here nor in the small grounds kept under control by someone who had no pretensions to being a gardener. The grass was cut but that was all. On my first day, I was placed in the fourth form, which was one below the Senior Cambridge examination form. I entered a large classroom of girls full of vitality and confidence. I sat quietly and 'kept my head down.' Most girls were indifferent to me and I preferred this to the hostility I had expected.

At break, four girls came round me wanting to know why I was there. As I suspected, they recognised me as going to the 'rival' school. Without any embroidering I told them how I came to be there, and the plain truth that I was pleased to have been accepted after the entrance examination. This satisfied them and so quickly I lost curiosity value. There was nothing in my story to cause resentment, incite jealousy or envy.

In life, there are some combinations one is simply not prepared for and Madam Racine was one. She neither walked nor ran, but did something in between and was from a mould completely outside my experience. I first met her when she rushed into our classroom one minute late, and moved to the blackboard with chalk in hand saying, 'Bonjour mes eleves.' The class rose, 'Bonjour Madame,' and sat down. As she wrote, she spoke in French. Common sense and the belated recognition of a word here and there gave me the impression that she was asking the girls about their holidays. Some of the girls were replying.

She saw me, nodded and smiled; I prayed to the gods that she would not ask me anything in French. My fear must have shown in my face. Then she lifted a pile of written work from the desk and said, 'This will not do. It just will not do. I am offended deeply.' Her anger was expressed in an accent which showed that she seldom spoke English. The class was silent. 'I was very disappointed by your class test. Now I have a proposal to put before you. This term, if you do not understand what I say, you will raise your hand like this (and she lifted her arm). If you do not understand and do not show your hand, I will understand that you prefer to be somewhere else, yes?'

The class was silent. 'This we can arrange between us, yes?' A nervous suppressed giggle came from somewhere.

That morning, she went over the end of term examination paper. I learnt that one's very best was expected, and failure to rise to those clearly-mapped heights provoked from Madam Racine the wrath of an Old Testament god. As she was about to step out of the classroom she turned her head and said, *'Demain une dictée. Ne me desappointez pas!'*

'What did she say?' I turned to Jean Fernandes.

'Dictation tomorrow.

Had I known someone willing to give me French *dictées* for the next twenty-four hours I would have left the classroom at once. That night I tried to get a French station on our enormous, dusty, grandfather radio which had an aerial on the roof and was grounded with a special wire (a protection against lightning I was told), but failed.

That day I was particularly quiet and attentive in all the morning classes, trying to do my best as a compensation for the humiliation which I knew lay ahead. How could I tell someone who spoke a foreign tongue and had no way of knowing whether I was speaking the truth that conversational French and dictées were unknowns to me? It would sound so implausible.

Then she came rushing in, her short hair flying. *'Bonjour mes eleves...'* she smiled.

Then on and on she went and would not stop. It was a French class but I had learnt French as if it were Latin. Something with grammar, syntax, vocabulary, irregular verbs but not something you would wish to speak.

Madame Racine read the passage. There was a pause. Now was the time to stand and explain that I had not done a *dictée* before. I had planned that I would go up to her before she began reading, but she started without warning. There was a studied silence hanging over the room and it suddenly seemed almost sacrilegious to puncture it with my voice. How could I explain that I had written French for two years but did not understand it when it was spoken; that I could read it to myself; that I had devised my own ways of overcoming this handicap to help me write it. Heaven forbid that she should ask me to give an example of what I was telling her.

How could I say all this to Madam Racine as she was poised to begin her *dictée* and demanding our undivided attention?

Time ticked on. I was listening intensely but heard sounds no one I knew ever made; sounds I could not spell. Phonetic spelling was out of the question. All I was sure about were the words for comma and full stop. The finality of Madam Racine's *'point'* was clear enough. At last it came to an end; the order given, 'Pass your books.' I felt diminished. I could not read what I had written. I had the beginnings of many words and the middle of a few. My common sense helped me but I was asking it to do the impossible. I needed more time to translate what I had written into plausible French, not necessarily the French of the *dictée* but a French!

'Hand me your book,' said Jean Fernandes, 'and stop writing now.' Jean Fernandes was good at French (but poor in mathematics I was delighted to discover) and full of an irritating something some people called 'style'. She shrugged her shoulders. I held on to my book. 'Pass me your book.' She spoke louder, trying to call attention to herself.

'No.' I said and dropped it inside my desk, bringing down the lid. Again she shrugged her shoulders in that unwholesome, irritating way. She lifted her eyebrows, moved her head and looked around her as searchlights do in prisoner-of-war camps. Was she seeing in my behaviour a deep, dark, undisciplined streak? I could take her unspoken attacks no more. I got up and walked towards my Goliath, unarmed.

Madame Racine's back was turned to the class. She was writing on the blackboard.

'Excuse me, Madam.' I said, almost in a whisper.

Without turning to see who it was she said, *'Excusez-moi s'il vous plait, Madame.'*

I said nothing and waited.

She turned and saw me. My face must have conveyed some of my distress and I heard myself say: 'I have not done a *dictée* before, Madam. I did not understand what you were saying and so I could not do it.'

'But I saw you writing.'

'I tried, Madam, but I could not manage it.'

'Let me see it.'

'I haven't done it, Madam.'

She looked at me and must have seen someone on the verge of crumbling. 'Very well. You are concerned about your work and that pleases me. That is the first essential step. Now, you have a long way to go with your spoken French, but if you are prepared to work there is nothing to stop you being competent in speaking.'

'Thank you, madam.'

'Merci, Madame s'il vous plait.'

'Merci, Madame Racine.'

Madame Racine loved being French. She made us feel that the French language was musical, sensitive, delicate and beautiful; it was the language of discretion and diplomacy. Gradually and unawares, I too began to see the French language through her eyes and listen to its rhythms and sounds through her warm vivacious personality. I was growing to understand that it was possible to say things in elegant and beautiful ways in another language; that having another language offered another human way of expressing one's self; that deep within its silken strands was another attitude, another way of thinking. I was becoming excited.

It was only when Madam Racine left after two terms that we realised how privileged we had been. Her husband was being stationed elsewhere. On the day she left I felt a deep inadequacy. I wanted to say to her in the finest most elegant French that not only was she an excellent French teacher but a wonderful human being. Instead I just stood up and joined the class in saying, *'Au revoir Madam Racine.'*

Everyone was excited about moving over to the new building and normally I too would have been, for the new SAGHS was a fine example of the new architecture: an architecture which was sensitive to psychic needs. There were large, picture windows which gave panoramic views of fields and sunlight. We were the beneficiaries of the new concept of letting the outside come within. Moreover, moving close to the Churchill-Roosevelt highway, with its own fine spacious grounds, meant that SAGHS had arrived.

But I was indifferent. I had grown to be at ease in the old, rambling, paint-flaking building. I was sorry to leave it, for in a strange sort of way, I felt that it had taken me in when I had no shelter.

But there were other more important, not so visible, changes the new building signified. In the past, girls who wanted a sound academic education had to travel all the way to the capital, Port of Spain. Even then, of the two finest girls' school there, only one, Bishop Anstey Girls' High School, taught some science subjects to Higher School Certificate level. And now here, for girls in the Tunapuna-St. Augustine-Curepe area, an area predominantly populated by rural East Indians, was a school right on their doorstep offering the most modern facilities for science.

In the 1950s science had the same aura and prestige as a brand new Rolls Royce of the latest model. In this new SAGHS building, science meant spacious rooms called laboratories with taps and sinks and glass dishes and burners and thin narrow tubes and high stools; all quite, quite different from the classrooms I knew of blackboard and chalk and duster. I remember walking along the corridors of those large new laboratories on open day with sadness, feeling that I was going to miss out on all this. It had arrived too late for us. We were, at fifteen, already too old to make a start, too old to become part of what was defined as the elixir of life.

St. Augustine Girls' High school was a happy place. This was true for all students irrespective of abilities or aptitudes. We were shown warmth and affection by the teachers, especially by the early 'founding' members who were visibly delighted when the work of weaker students was improving. There was also a strong desire to lift the academic standing of this newly created school to a par with the long established girls' schools in Port of Spain, the schools which took the top prizes – the girls' island scholarships – more frequently than most.

SAGHS had the advantages of youth: energy and an optimistic belief in the future. It was willing to give everyone a chance: both teachers and students. As a result, we had many young, untried, but lively teachers.

There was one young woman with the charm of an ambitious politician. She was popular with the class and did not see the need to separate the chaff from the wheat, and seemed to think that if students could but only spin many pages, this chaff would, of its own accord, turn into grains of wheat. The marks she gave reflected this personal belief.

Another bright young woman, straight from University, lectured to us instead of teaching; she must have felt that we had the ability to pick out the meaningful and the useful from her forty minute lecture. Not being able to do this, we were instead impressed by her style and admired the ease with which she could say things we did not understand. She was held in high regard.

And skilful teaching is not synonymous with age. We had a dear dedicated teacher who was so keen that we should have a thorough understanding of our subject that much time was spent on the reading of fine explanatory notes and the study of yet finer notes on fine notes. In the process many forgot what the main text had to say and so its spirit was elegantly smothered by elaborate pedantry.

154

But there was also Mrs. Chan our mathematics teacher, who had the ability to teach mathematics to anyone prepared to pay attention to her step-by-step approach. She dressed simply, almost casually. Her short hair, like a new mop, had much spring and was kept out of the way by a hair clip. She moved backward and forward logically in her expositions (her arms and legs following in unison), reminding the slow amongst us where and how she had derived the knowns and with great clarity used the knowns to unravel the unknowns. It was so prettily done, so elegantly and neatly formulated that it excited me. I saw geometry and algebra as being challenging riddles with their own built-in keys to solution and would of my own accord spend many a Sunday afternoon solving geometry riders rather than go to the matinee show at the local cinema.

In the summer of 1954 SAGHS opened its exit door for the second time in its history to its successful students: those who had acquired the passport to jobs, the Senior Cambridge School Certificate.

The school still had a long way to go before it gained an honoured place for its academic standing; nevertheless I felt that SAGHS was an important part of a quiet revolution taking place amongst the East Indian population which they, as well as everyone else, seemed to be taking for granted.

Many of the students came from homes where parents had not had a primary school education; homes with traditional Hindu mothers, conservative women, whose own marriages had been arranged, but who were now giving their daughters a freedom undreamt of in their own childhood. Few schools could claim to fill their classrooms with such speed. Throughout the northern breadth of Trinidad, girls of East Indian descent came pouring into SAGHS as if it were a colossal magnet.

It is difficult to say exactly what caused this rapid change. Just a few years earlier most parents were doubtful about the relevance of algebra and Latin to a Hindu girl with good marriage prospects. My uncle, you may recall, would not send his elder daughter Parbatee to FGHS and sent her instead to

155

the Archibald Institute where she learnt the varied and valuable arts and skills necessary to organise a healthy and happy home. Now he sent his second daughter to SAGHS as if it were a matter of course.

Whether it was the effect of the general release of women's energies after the second World War, seeping southwards from the Northern Hemisphere; whether it was the influence of the United States with its sturdy dollar and its 'reach for the skies' philosophy; or whether parents and their daughters could see the opportunities that women's economic participation gave to the home, I cannot say; but these were times when it became less difficult for an educated young woman to carry on a full time job and be a good mother and wife. In her own mother (and mother-in-law if she were lucky) there was invariably help in emergencies, while home-help was more readily available and at a price attractive to a young graduate.

Inevitably there were casualties of this new freedom.

Some of the girls were unable to appreciate fully its true value and the very real opportunities it was providing. They did not see themselves in a new role. Others, coming from sheltered homes, were ill-equipped to cope with the many allurements of their new found freedom, like the flattery of bold, clever young men. There were unsuitable connections and associations formed too early, but the vast majority grappled successfully with their new situation and showed that young women, whatever their culture, however conservative their home background, were endowed with the resources to climb great heights in whatever field they chose.

And so it was that this gigantic glacier of tradition and conservatism had begun to thaw. I saw ten year olds move easily from one culture to another, from rolling out *roties* in the morning, cooking on a *chulha* with wood from the forest, to making careful written observations through a microscope an hour later. It convinced me that the human mind had the capacity to move from rural to urban; from swimming near the seashore to exploring the ocean's deep canyons – and the galaxies above, all in one generation.

Over the years I continued to massage my grandmother, whenever her back pained her. I thought nothing of it, for these massages were meant to bring her a little ease, which they did. It was only when Savitri, Tara's daughter, was getting married that I was forced to think of a massage other than as a means of easing pain. And there was another matter; looking closely at my grandmother, I saw the female body as the place where pain and stress resided, a receptacle for the accumulated buffetings of life. In the preparations for Savitri's wedding, I was encouraged to think of a woman's body differently, as a bower of comfort and pleasure.

According to custom, a bride-to-be was thoroughly massaged a few days before the wedding with a special freshly-prepared mixture of oil and herbs, and the masseuses had to be three young Brahmin maidens. My mother did not tell me exactly what was expected of me, she merely said that Tara would explain it all.

It was pleasant meeting my cousin Sati, and Uma, a close family friend. They had done this before and knew what it entailed. Uma was the niece of a pundit and was keen on expounding the significance of everything.

'Come now,' Tara said.

All three of us followed her into the outdoor bathroom where we found Savitri smiling coyly, wrapped in a towel and seated on a *peerha*. I smiled too.

'Look who I brought to give you a good massage and make your skin glow,' her mother said.

We all giggled and were handed a bowl of finely ground saffron sticks mixed with olive oil and many scented herbs. Tara spoke. 'Now take a little at a time like this. Time to remove that towel, Savitri.' Reluctantly Savitri uncovered herself and I saw that she was naked. I was not prepared for this.

Savitri bent her head and I looked at the wall behind her.

'Now you all stop being shy. You are like sisters, you have been brought up together. You are like family; nothing to be ashamed about. Look. Like this....' and Tara rubbed the golden yellow mixture firmly into her daughter's back.

'I am going to leave you all now. A little later *Sadhuayin* will come and see how you're managing. Take care and don't let it drop on your clothes.' She parted the door of dried coconut leaves and left.

'I will do my face and neck; Kamla, you do the back. Sati will do the hands and Uma the feet,' said Savitri. In the absence of her mother she seemed to have lost her shyness. We became serious professionals. Not a square centimetre escaped us. We were here to do a job. Uma, the eldest and a tough, hard-working young woman, set the tone and Sati and I followed. In silence, we rubbed this rich sunshine mix into Savitri's skin. I noticed Savitri did her inner thighs and bottom too. I didn't think that was necessary, but felt there was no accounting for idiosyncrasies. I kept my thoughts to myself.

So Savitri was massaged from her forehead to her toes until she looked like a golden girl. The *Sadhuayin* came. She brought a special rich *dahi* mix for Savitri's hair. 'Alright, you have done a very good job. Should I recommend you as a team?' she asked, smiling. 'Thank you. Now I have my job to do.'

Tara gave us soap and a scrubber to wash our hands, but the rich yellow would not go.

'Not to worry in a day or two – it will take a little time – but it will go,' she said, and went into the kitchen, returning with three bowls of creamy *kheer*.

'You have to be paid,' she said, 'after working so hard.' We were delighted to be offered these steaming bowls with the aroma of hot *kheer*, cinnamon and nutmeg; but we all said, 'Oh no, *Mamee*, you shouldn't have taken so much trouble. You mean all that trouble *you* went into? You are really spoiling us now.' We were fast learning the ways of adults. Tara said, 'This is no trouble. It is my pleasure, my privilege, my blessing to have three fine young Brahmin ladies come here to assist me.' We listened and I wanted to believe her.

As we three walked down the road in the direction of my home, I thought aloud. 'What does that do to your skin?'

'Makes it yellow,' said Sati, grinning. 'Just look at your hands.'

'What else?' I asked.

'The old people say it makes your skin beautifully soft and moist and adds a glow. It is an old-fashioned beauty treatment. It goes back well before the Queen of Sheba. It must have come from the Indus valley of 3000 BC.'

'Who says it is that ancient?' I queried.

Uma said, 'Look, these things came from India and they were handed down for generations.'

'Does it work? That's the important question,' I remarked.

'Does cold cream work? Does vanishing cream work? Who knows? That's just like you, Kamla. You don't question whether vanishing cream works, but you question whether saffron works. That comes from having too much of a Western education.'

'I don't use cold cream.'

'You don't use vanishing cream either?'

'Very, very seldom.'

'Very seldom or not, you use it, and that's my point.'

'I don't see why we have to quarrel.'

'Who is quarrelling? I am not quarrelling. I am making a point that needs to be made. Far, far too often, Western educated girls are too quick to criticise Hindu things, but they are not criticising Western things. They are very objective when it comes to the inheritance of their forefathers but when it comes to western things their power of criticism loses its teeth.'

'I hope you're not referring to me, because I want to learn from both sides.'

'You can't serve both sides.'

'I didn't say serve.'

'I know you didn't. But you will have to serve one side or the other.'

'I am not ready to serve anything yet. Like my father said, I have a lot to learn.'

'We all have. But some only learn what they want to learn, not what there is to learn.'

'Look, stop this I don't want to quarrel over nothing.'

'It wasn't nothing. You were questioning our traditional beauty treatment for brides.'

'I merely asked whether it was effective.'

'Yes. But isn't that the same thing? You see, no one, absolutely no one questions whether the bottled beauty treatments in the drug store are effective. Who goes to the druggist and picks up something and says, "Excuse me, Mr. Charles, is this effective?" No they don't. They merely read what it says on the bottle and believe it.'

I was pleased to reach home for I was upset at what Uma had said. What she had said was true. Why didn't I question the beauty treatments in the drug store? Was it because of the advertisements on the radio, in the newspapers, and on large poster boards? We believed the advertisements. I did not think then that anyone would dare to say something untrue so often in public. I knew it was also because these products were very attractively packaged and they came from countries we believed to be highly scientific and advanced. This worried me. We were all buying on trust. We had no way of knowing. Perhaps, I thought, next time I met Uma I would say to her, 'Why don't you bottle this ancient beauty treatment and call it "The Queen of Sheba",' but after thinking of what her response might be, I dropped the idea.

ORANGES AND ORCHIDS

At the time I was there, in June 1954, SAGHS did not yet offer its successful Senior Cambridge students an opportunity to take the Higher School Certificate – this was to come later – and so once again I turned to St. Joseph's Convent in Port of Spain and made an application to join their well-established Higher School Certificate class.

In many ways St. Joseph's Convent was a contrast to SAGHS. It was not in the middle of fields, open to the cooling trade winds descending from the Northern Range. It was, instead, situated in the capital, in the main port, retailing, administrative and commercial centre of the island.

However, it stood hemmed in by its own high walls which also protected it from the dust and noise of the city. Its architecture was solid, secure, and ecclesiastical, declaring its authority and separation from the outer world and its close affiliation with the church which controlled the inner designs of its teaching.

It stood opposite the Catholic school for boys, the College of the Immaculate Conception, popularly called St. Mary's. That also had the same heavy solidity, the weightiness of much columnar concrete.

In the 1830s the planners of St. Joseph's Convent would have wanted it to be outside the city, and they had chosen well; even one hundred and twenty years later it was still on the periphery of the city's energy, though gradually being encroached upon by the city's outward growth. So, St. Joseph's had always been well away from the rattling of horses and carts, buggies and tram cars; away from the loading of cargo in and out of warehouses; the trucks packed high with white bags of Canadian flour; jute bags of rice from British Guiana and bulging net bags of onions and Irish potatoes; tinned milk and milk powder; corned beef from Argentina and salt fish from Newfoundland; barrels of mackerel in brine; molasses and twelve-inch-long bars of blue and deep brown soap and the paler 'family' soap.

It had always been well away from the black smoke of: steam trains arriving from the countryside, their carriages filled with school children and fresh vegetables; from the clerks and shoppers and traders; from ambitious men too neatly dressed, hurrying away from the common multitude to sedate jobs, with colleagues who spoke of higher ambitions openly and carelessly.

It had been well away from all the dust and smells of living.

The Convent was situated in the quiet elegant northern part of Port of Spain with its Queen's Park Savannah, encircled by great houses and fine buildings: the Botanic Gardens, the Governor's House, Queen's Royal College, neighbouring specialist libraries and squares of flowering shrubs and trees. All these made it possible to imagine the more gracious life style of the few in the dark age of slavery. By 1954 offices and private houses had, helter-skelter, linked hands and surrounded St. Joseph's. But except for impatient car drivers, the noise of the city scarcely penetrated that far into Pembroke Street and was unable to scale the Convent's walls.

In September of 1954 I started at St. Joseph's, and like other country children entered the city by train. Later as I walked along Frederick Street I saw my childhood mirrored in the shops. There was Staubles, the patisserie shop with its high stools onto which I had to be helped by my mother, with the same inviting smells flowing out onto the pavement. I could not see the jams and jellies wrapped in flaky Danish pastry of my childhood, but there were pretty cakes and ice cream sundaes on display. I passed the shop where my mother tested the wool content of suiting material; the optician where I was given my first pair of glasses and the ugly decaying building where a smiling old man and his son were amongst the finest of dentists; something I did not know then and would never have known had I not been told it by the dental teaching department of a British university.

As I walked towards St. Joseph's Convent, the school over which I had wept at my exclusion two years earlier, I felt unsure of myself. I entered by the narrow south gate half-expecting that someone would challenge my right to be there. But there was no one at the gate. It was early and I was surprised at the ease with which one could simply walk in. The few boarders present from Venezuela said nothing to me. I was wearing the school uniform and was one of them.

I stepped lightly across the yard, along the very clean, deep reddish-brown tiles of the corridor, and was surprised to find a fountain in a small square which, years later, I realised would not have looked out of place in a school in Rome.

From the very first day, I could see that the nuns who would be teaching us were very familiar with the route to obtaining the Higher School Certificate. They had walked that path many times before, with other girls, and would now be taking us the same way. Their methods were of the past: traditional, unexciting and suited only to the very bright. They wasted no time and started the syllabus immediately. St. Joseph's did not offer any of the Sciences, Mathematics or History at Higher School Certificate level. It offered French, Spanish and Latin; English Literature and Geography. Except for the last, a subject I always enjoyed, I could see from the very first lesson that the standards these girls had attained were higher than my own.

Once again French returned to haunt me. When I left Fatima Girls' High School and entered SAGHS I had to drop Spanish as it was not offered. This was a substantial loss as Mother Anthony was good in Spanish and we had almost completed the Senior Cambridge syllabus. Unfortunately, when Madame Racine left SAGHS, the French class suffered a great deal and the true extent of this I was only to discover with the French nun, Mere Marie. I dropped French at once for I did not wish to have nightmares over *dictées* and conversational French.

English literature at Higher School Certificate level was a grand thing to do. It entailed the study of eleven text books whereas for my Senior Cambridge I had done a mere two or three. Of the poets, I liked Wordsworth, Milton and Shelley; and I was deeply moved by Matthew Arnold's 'Sohrab and Rustum' and felt as if I too had stood on the brink of the yellow Oxus and shared Rustum's deep anguish.

For a school whose pupils had been studying English literature for decades I was surprised that there was no proper library for Higher School Certificate girls, though there was a place called 'the library'. It was a room downstairs: clean, polished and serene, an area of privilege which only Higher School Certificate girls were allowed to use. But though there were neat, fine-looking book cases with glass doors along the

163

walls, few people borrowed anything from them. The books, though beautifully bound, were weighty and forbidding and of no relevance to what we were studying. Nevertheless, the library became a place of study for our free periods and I was impressed that, for most of the time, girls behaved responsibly and it was truly a place for reflection.

It was there that Sir Walter Scott brought the clans of Scotland alive for me; I rode through the glens and crossed streams and wild country; took sides and hid in castles, looking from watchtowers for approaching horsemen and waging surprise attacks. But alas, literature was not solely for my enjoyment; I had to pass an exam. I had to have views and opinions about characters and what authors meant. I knew that at times I said things I did not mean, and wondered to what extent characters in books did the same. I felt inadequate and unable to give an opinion about a writer or a people or a time of which I knew so little. Over the years I had come to realise that my opinions were usually not shared by others. I did not believe in the objectivity of examiners but was sure *they* were clear in their own minds as to what *were* the correct interpretations. My problem lay in not knowing what these were. I had learnt not to express in public what my inner voice was saying and had no intention of exposing my opinions in writing; so I walked a mile to the specialist library, White Hall, overlooking the Queen's Park Savannah, in search of the opinions of men and women who were considered fine critics. When I could not find their views on things I wished to know, I was in a quandary.

At the end of my first year we were told that the literature books we had completed would be revised in a general class revision nearer our examination. I was looking forward to this, believing that the teacher's opinions were a guide to the accepted viewpoints, particularly those held by the examiners. Unfortunately it never took place and we were never warned it was not going to take place. This negligence created so much anxiety in me that for many years after, whenever I was troubled about anything, my nightmare took the form of having to thoroughly revise eleven books in two months. Then in a speedy and mysterious way, the time span would be reduced, though the number of books to be revised remained constant; so eventually there would be eleven books to revise in eleven days, then ten days, nine days and so on, right up to one day; and I would be busily engaged trying to divide this one day into eleven equal parts: all this time finding I could not recall anything about any of the books....

So, unsure, confused and ill-at-ease amongst teachers I never grew to know, and whose traditional teaching methods neither enlightened nor excited me, my two years at St. Joseph's Convent came to an end in the summer of 1956.

But there was one thing left: the end of school party. I was at first surprised, then gently amused, to learn that we could invite young men. I wondered how the nuns had arrived at this decision, for a recent classroom discussion with Mother Paul had remained with me. It was during the current affairs period. Our regular teacher was absent and Mother Paul took her place. How exactly the subject of sex before marriage came to the fore I cannot tell, except to say that in our last few days at school the atmosphere in the classroom was very relaxed and we were all displaying a lively, noisy *laisser-faire* spirit.

One brave girl, Jean Akai, wanted to know if an elderly couple, very much in love and engaged to be married, who found that for financial reasons they had to postpone marrying, whether under such circumstances of fine intent and where, perhaps, time was of the essence, whether the Church would allow.....' Jean was not permitted to land her craft; for Mother Paul saw through the camouflage and there came a strong warning: 'Do not go gently down that path...' She paused. 'The Church's teaching is quite clear, Jean. You know this. It is there to protect you. Marriage is a large, difficult, serious undertaking. You need the sacrament of holy matrimony to assist you from the start. Be wise. Be patient.' The class shuffled uneasily and Mother Paul felt that she had not made the right impression. She tried again. 'What does one do with an orange after sucking it?' As we looked at her, sitting erect, statuesque and dignified, an uncanny, uncomfortable hush filled the room. Again she posed the question, 'What does one do with an orange that is sucked dry?' I sucked oranges, we all did, but the question did not make sense, and we were silent, awaiting an explanation or a clue. 'Come on. What do you do?'

'Throw it away,' Elisabeth Jay said; and we laughed at the silly honesty of her reply.

'Precisely. It is discarded, it is thrown away without any ceremony. It is simply dropped into the nearest bin or rubbish heap. No one has need for what is left.' And then with a wide sweeping movement of her right hand, Mother Paul threw an imaginary orange, sucked dry, through the open window. She did it with such vehemence that sitting there in that upstairs class room, we all waited to hear it fall.

So, I puzzled, remembering Mother Paul's stance, boys would be allowed to enter this hallowed place, this female fortress; the enemy stands outside the gates and yet the drawbridge is being lowered. There must be more to it. I guessed at the arguments which had gone on in the staff room. 'We the sisters of Cluny of St Joseph,' said one side, 'ought not to put temptations in the way of our young girls, so vulnerable, so susceptible in these impressionable years.' And the other: 'To conduct themselves properly in the company of young men, unchaperoned, is something our girls will have to learn; why not take this opportunity to present a party atmosphere and by our own conduct, give guidance as to how healthy enjoyment is created.'

Except for a few of us in our year of twenty-four who said they did not know whom to invite, the girls were excited about the party. During break, there were long-drawn-out discussions as to whether 'he' would come if invited or whether it were better to play safe and invite 'him' who could be so boring. I decided that I would not be coming. There was a young man whose sister I knew well and whom I met daily on the school bus (I travelled by bus in my second year) but I did not wish him to think that I favoured him. I later changed my mind and joined the group of four girls who had decided that although they would not be inviting a young man, they would be coming to the class party which we saw as a celebration of the end of school life and the beginning of adulthood.

With the help of the nuns the room allocated to us was modestly decorated. Savouries, sweets, soft drinks and cider were provided on a side table, covered with a well-starched white cotton tablecloth.

The more sophisticated you were, the later you came and accompanied by a young man. I came on time as did the others in the group of four. The room was far larger than our numbers warranted and even when all had arrived, there was too much space between us for the growth of a common warmth and jollity. As I sipped a warm soft drink, keeping close to the wall for protection, I observed the different levels of sophistication, maturity and worldliness amongst us. Without the common mask of our school uniform, individualities were being unveiled.

There were girls like Meera and Savitri who knew how to make themselves attractive by their carriage, their clothes and hair styles. They moved with an easy triumphant air. There were others whose dress was guided by maternal care, a care that would not be taken in by rapidly changing flights of fancy, preferring what had stood the test of time and served the values of modesty and maidenhood. These girls, on the verge of adulthood, were still dressed in the outgrown styles of childhood: in high round necklines, gently gathered waist-lines, puffed sleeves and substantial bows, tied at the back. They reminded me in their simplicity and innocence of the hibiscus flower. But we also had in our midst, the exotic orchids who were already attracting the bees, butterflies and the appraising eyes of bystanders as well as those who had other engagements.

The nuns popped in now and then. I was happy to see this and would have liked them to stay longer, for I sensed in some a warm, merry, almost childlike fervour for the party, hidden beneath their long apparel.

167

As the evening wore on, everyone was looking forward to the arrival of the music, so there was a feeling of exhilaration when the gramophone was brought in.

But I was never at ease with modern Western dance. It entailed aspects of physical contact that were contrary to my upbringing: I had to allow my entire hand to be held by a complete stranger, but that was not all; I had to permit him to be uncomfortably close to me and pretend it were not so. In addition I would have to compromise further and say nothing when he placed his arm around my waist while I rested my other hand on his shoulder. It was a posture that would be frowned upon in my village as full of mischief. To have a stranger stand that close to me assailed my notion of self. I had always felt the need to have space around me, more so with strangers in a hot room. I did not desire to be jostled, to be guided or to be led – with or without the aid of music – and neither did I wish to make believe I was enjoying myself. I felt it might be alright for Christians to see this as an innocent pleasure, but my Hindu upbringing would not compromise with such a stance.

After a little tussle as to which record should be played first, the music started. Those with partners needed no encouragement. Some whose partners had not yet arrived danced together. Those without partners crowded round the gramophone and created a role for themselves in selecting records and placing them in one order and then in another and went about offering choices to those with other interests.

I knew it was time for me to leave. All I wanted to do was to slip away quietly, unnoticed. I thought of the clear brook with the talking fishes: and I saw myself just sitting there embraced by the wind and the sound of falling water and the smell of long grass. I went downstairs; quietly closed the door behind me and faced the cool night air.

I walked down Pembroke Street, a displaced person between two worlds whose rules of etiquette were foreign one to another. Here, in this urban Western setting, having a boyfriend and being able to dance in the manner I have described were assets. In the place I was walking towards, my home, my village, such behaviour would be regarded as uncouth, unladylike, sullied and sullying. When I reached Frederick Street, the city's smells of oranges, open drains, urine, car exhausts, beggars, syrup, shoe boxes, bales of cloth and parched nuts, awakened me from my reverie; I quickened my steps to the bus terminus in Henry Street.

CHASED AND TRAPPED

For reasons I cannot explain my mind became active at nights. Two dreams not connected with hell (though its unquenchable fires raged too) remained with me throughout my childhood. But if I can't explain what provoked the bouts of dreaming, their sources are clear enough.

Our hens had a preference for laying eggs under the house. And so, from time to time, my mother sent me with an enormous enamel bowl to collect them. The house of my childhood was slightly raised from the ground, by wooden stilts about twelve inches high. There was only one narrow entrance which the hens used and which I too had to use. Light entered this dark, dusty, feathered plain through two narrow rectangular vents which were covered by wire netting that had to be mended at times to prevent snakes and rats from entering. Once we discovered a snake, a yard long, curled up behind several jute bags of rice and sugar in our shop.

It wasn't difficult to find the eggs because our hens were birds of habit. They had, with time, worn for themselves comfortable cavities in the earth. These were so deep, it was impossible to tell what was inside them, until you were right up to them. They were deep enough, I thought, for a medium sized snake to curl into. This fear I kept to myself. The eggs were needed; they were good for you; everyone said so. But alas! no one but I could squeeze into that narrow opening and crawl on my stomach like a swimming frog.

There was also Mr. Mohammed's bull, Abdull. The Mohammeds, our next door neighbours, kept cows, and as we did not, the grass in front of our house was always lush and overgrown, especially during the rainy season. Mr. Mohammed and his son started to tether their cows and young bull in front of our house, and because we did not complain, they planted their thick iron tethering rod closer and yet closer to the entrance of our front gate.

My parents did not mind but I was unhappy about this and my fears materialised one day when, arriving from school, I found their bull blocking my path to our front gate. I stood at a distance and made strange guttural sounds and waved my arms about, but this mammoth would not be moved. He munched on and on like a combine harvester, looking up from time to time to see if I was still there.

I needed to go to the bathroom and felt more and more uncomfortable. When I finally managed to slip inside, I complained bitterly to my mother. Next day she asked Mrs. Mohammed to tether the young bull in such a way that I would feel safe. Mrs. Mohammed did not take kindly to this request. She could vouch that Abdull would not hurt anyone if not molested. She had never had a single complaint before. By the time she had finished protesting, I was made to feel that I was unreasonable and selfish, denying Abdull what I couldn't use.

And so it was, one night, as I lay under the mosquito net, I dreamt I was being chased by that very bull, now transformed into a bison. Round and round the savannah he chased me with his head bent, his enormous body pounding the earth close behind me. I could feel his breathing getting closer, and saw his nose dilating and slaver dripping from his mouth. I ran for all I was worth.

Then I remembered the one tree in this broad savannah, but it was too far away, so I had to wait until I ran round the savannah again. The bull seemed to realise exactly what I was thinking and began to close in on me. It was nearly all over for me when I found a burst of energy, and just had time to scramble up the first branch. The bull could not check himself and I was able to climb to the higher safer branches. He was so enraged to see this that he charged again and again, butting the trunk of the tree and using his two fore legs to dig into the roots. At first I felt quite safe, even though the branches were shaking violently; then the trunk itself began to heave this way and that. But just before the tree fell I found that I could fly.

My arms lifted me and like a small two-seater plane I soared upwards. When I looked down I saw the fallen tree and began to feel safe again; I was enjoying the sensation of flying with the wind against my hair and face. But when I looked down I was puzzled that I couldn't see the bull in the savannah. I looked behind and there he was, also flying and smiling in a wily superior way. Now, he looked a little like Miss Medina's cow that jumped over the moon.

I decided to fly homewards towards the open yard of my home. There I landed. To my relief he could not descend as I did. He circled twice but could not land. It was as if some strong magic was protecting the space around our house.

I opened my eyes and saw familiar things and was happy to find myself in bed; but not long after, there I am creeping under the house to collect the eggs. As soon as I reach halfway, the entire house slides downwards, the stilts grow shorter and shorter and I am pinned stomach-down like a frog sprawled flat after being run over at night. I try to wriggle out, but I am firmly pinned down. I begin to feel claustrophobic. I try to shout, to scream, but my mouth is squashed into the earth. I am crying out but my sounds are too muffled, too feeble. I can hear noises from outside. They drown me, they suffocate me. I am like the frog.

Again I cry out, but it seems now I cannot cry – a great difficulty – a most unnatural one falls upon me and I know that I can never move nor scream again. Fear explodes within me for my condition is a hopeless one – pinned between house and earth for ever.

Then the morning sun comes in through a chink; I am in bed; the hens cluck and move about waiting to be fed; the wheels of early bullock carts turn and I am so relieved, so thankful, so full of joy, so happy to be able to move, to stand, to walk; and I know that these are all miraculous things and I am blessed.

PART FIVE

STANDING ON THE OTHER SIDE

teacher

I was now on the other side of the teacher's desk; I had become the 'Miss' for Standard Two at Tunapuna Mahasabha Primary school. I couldn't help thinking of my days in Miss Medina's class. 'Please keep your desks in a neat row,' I heard myself say.

The school functioned on an 'open plan' and my teaching methods and my ability to manage the class were in full view of older more experienced heads (including the difficult-to-please Headmaster), younger ones fresh from the Government Teachers' Training College and all the pupils. I felt greatly exposed, for much was expected from Higher School Certificate graduates.

I prepared my lessons as well as I could and tried not to become angry when provoked by older boys in the back row. These boisterous lads would try to recapture the highlights of a local cricket match or some excitement in the village, while I stood before the blackboard explaining how relief rainfall was triggered off on our Northern Range. There was also an element of 'showmanship'. You knew that other teachers would be looking critically at your blackboard, so my earth was not simply round as a ball, it was more like an orange, flattened slightly at the top and the bottom. As my blackboard said: the earth is an oblate spheroid.

Fortunately it was possible to escape outside to the nearby savannah where we were allowed to take our classes for poetry or reading or nature study. There we had the shade of three large pink flowering immortelle trees to choose from. There I was more relaxed with my class, and they with me.

175

But there came another distraction; his name was Surinder. Slim, intelligent, radical and wayward with an enormous amount of vitality, a fine all rounder at cricket, I had noticed him before but never consciously focused on anything but the needs of my class. This single-mindedness was not to last long. Mrs. Jasmin Moustafa's class and Mr. Surinder Singh's were side by side. One afternoon on my way home she told me, 'That young Surinder is crazy about you. Haven't you noticed? Those eyes of his, he cannot keep them away from you. Such an able, fine young man. I know his family well. What a distinguished-looking father. He sits on the Board you know.' How does one respond to such observations from a middle-aged woman with grown-up children? My life so far had tasted little of this heady wine. It might even have been my initial lack of interest that made Mrs. Moustafa, a born matchmaker, feel more keenly than ever that she had a part to play. And just as soft drops of water will, with time, leave their mark even on granite, Mrs. Moustafa's soft flatteries brought about a change in me. My former peace of mind, my independence, my freedom of thought were beginning to weaken. I discovered that I was taking particular care with my toilet. One day I happened to be early and to my surprise so too was Surinder. I acknowledged his presence at the entrance with a very formal 'Good Morning.' My tone would have given the impression that I was grooming myself to be the Headmaster. In a tropical white cotton blouse, cream Irish linen skirt and well brushed shoulder-length hair, I walked the length of the building feeling acutely ill-at-ease for I felt his eyes upon me. In my classroom I busied myself with getting the coloured chalk from the cupboard, straightening the desks and studying the day's timetable. I sat down feeling warm and uncomfortable and, after what seemed like eternity, lifted my eyes from an arithmetic exercise book and saw him still looking in my direction. I gave my customary slight nod and then it was that he smiled in such a warm, appealing, contagious manner that I too quite involuntarily smiled without restraint. His eyes gleamed and his hair laughed and he seemed to have brightened the entire building. All that day my mind was like a butterfly and in order to concentrate better I took my class outside under the pink immortelles.

I was committed to my class and had grown fond of these spirited, receptive boys and girls, thirty-five in number. They were not considered high-fliers. Those with that stamp were placed in Mrs. Moustafa's class from age seven to eight. Two years later the privileged ones would be well-prepared for the highly competitive island-wide examination known as the Government exhibition – having had successive years of thorough grounding with Surinder and the Headmaster. The successful candidates were well rewarded with free secondary school education in the island's finest schools. The Tunapuna Mahasabha Primary school did very well in these examinations and in this way its reputation was enhanced.

I wanted the boys and girls in my class to have a good year while I was with them (perhaps unconsciously I wished to be their Madam Racine) and so my lack of concentration on that day when Surinder smiled disturbed me.

Throughout the 1940s and 1950s the East Indian population in Trinidad grew rapidly. At this time came the Mahasabha movement, men and women concerned that Trinidad Indians should become more fully conscious of the educational facilities on the island and of the rich inheritance of Indian classical dance, music, song and literature. It was felt that the more traditional, difficult and profound aspects of Indian culture were being neglected and their place taken by both Indian and Western popular culture displayed daily on our cinema screens.

The Tunapuna Mahasabha Primary school, opened in September 1952, was one of the first fruits of this courageous movement. In addition to its cultural aims, it broke the monopoly encouraged by the colonial practice of state support only for Christian schools in a multiracial, multicultural society. At morning assembly, prayers were said in Sanskrit and sacred songs sung in Sanskrit too. I had been taught seventeenth century English ditties and beautiful old English songs and sad, soul-moving Negro spirituals at the Tunapuna Government Primary school; but there was no place for anything Indian. It was here at the Tunapuna Mahasabha Primary school that I had the opportunity to learn a little more about my ancient and rich cultural heritage. I soon grew to love the solemn Sanskrit hymns and tranquil chants, and added them to my repertoire of beautiful Latin chants I had unconsciously absorbed during my Catholic school days.

The development which had culminated in the formation of the Mahasabha movement had been stimulated by India's achievement of independence. That event did much to encourage Indians in Trinidad to resist the denigration of anything not European.

In my school atlas the British Empire was represented in pink and it looked as if pink ink had accidentally been spilt on every continent in the world. Now, after 1947, that colour would have to be removed from the subcontinent of India. This was of great psychic importance to Indians in Trinidad. It should have been of equal importance to all non-white races in British colonial Trinidad; but sadly we were a people already divided amongst ourselves.

I joined a group of Tunapuna primary school children organised by the Headmaster of the evening school – the Tunapuna Hindi school. We were taught the first stanzas of India's national songs and so, with the national flag of India in our hands, we waved the yellow, white and green colours as we marched in a neat long column from Tunapuna to Curepe on India's Independence day.

When we arrived I was surprised to find so many other columns of young Indians awaiting us; and as our column marched in, there were other columns of school children singing and making the call millions in India were making to the last of a long line of conquerors: *'Doora tho Doora tho Hindustan Hamara hai.'* We sang with our hearts, our heads and our hands.

I had never seen so many Indian children together in one place before. I had seen columns of ants in our garden and columns of Roman soldiers marching into captured cities in vast panoramic scenes in the cinema; on this day I felt I had become a part of just such a grand spectacle. I was elated and moved to stand with hundreds of other young people celebrating the miraculous.

'Miraculous': that was my father's word. The night before the march he said to me:

'Look at it this way. In India you will find very poor people, people without a formal education. Untutored. The mass of Indians are poor, millions have died in famines while the British were there and no doubt it will take time before there is enough for all. And yet what have those ordinary men and women done? They have accomplished the impossible. They have forced a people who colonised them for 300 years to leave. It was the mightiest Empire of recent times; and yet with all its military grandeur, its false arrogance, its machinery of educated men in London, full of their own importance and of the images they had created of themselves and of us all; these men were overthrown, not by Western methods but by an essential Indian method of *Satyagraha* – mass civil disobedience. India's Independence is a great human achievement. It is an achievement of statesmen over politicians, an achievement of the spirit of the common man over false overlords. Now would you have thought that possible? Would you have thought that you too were living in times of great hope for mankind? The large struggles of life are not confined to the *Ramayana* or the *Mahabharata*.'

I could not respond to what my father had said. I did not know how to.

And there in the midst of that grand gathering I saw a three year old standing to attention, in broken sandals, as thin as a grain of rice, singing with all the energy he could muster:

Vande Mataram!
Sujalam, sulphalam, malayaja-shitalam,
Shasyashyamalam, Mataram!

I bow to thee, Mother,
richly-watered, richly-fruited,
cool with the winds of the South,
dark with the crop of the harvests, the Mother!

Then came a short speech on the beautiful, essential thing Freedom was, and of the great responsibility we children had to carry this bright torch to the next generation. The whole gathering of children then burst into Rabindranath Tagore's song:

Jana-gana-mana-adhinayakajaya he
Bharata-bhagya-vidhata.

Thou art the ruler of the minds of all people,
Dispenser of India's destiny.

Before me, this slender grain of rice, with the sun and a wisp of hair in his eyes, sang with such youthful assurance that I wept for the supreme courage of the weak; and I wept too for those daring dauntless runaway slaves who never made it; and for the heroism and valour of the Red Indians of North America who did not have India's good fortune. Not for the first time in my life, as this stanza of Tagore's song came to an end, I felt a deep kinship with the courage of the vanquished.

After the school year ended in July, I attended the Primary School Teachers' annual conference which was held in our school. Most of the teachers of our school were attending as the headmaster had made it clear that listening to the experiences of others was important. On each day, a number of subject papers were read and participants willingly told of their teaching problems and how they had tried to solve them. Imagine my surprise when, on the final day, a method of teaching long division, which I had already used with Standard Two, was presented as a paper. I was excited that someone felt the method was of sufficient value to be published. I'd kept my method to myself for I had no way of evaluating it and none of the older teachers had commented on it. I was very happy, but resisted the temptation to tell anyone that morning. In the afternoon, however, Surinder came and sat near to me; it was the last day we would be together.

'Looking forward to going to England?' he asked.

'Yes. I have no idea what it will be like. But I am excited.' Then I couldn't resist saying, 'Do you know that I already used the method to teach long division that we were shown this morning?'

'Yes, I remember seeing it on your blackboard. I came over to congratulate you really,' and he stretched out his hand. I hesitated at first, then held it. I was surprised that fingers that had turned cricket balls and hands that had firmly held the bat should be so sensitive. I held his hands far longer than I should, seconds longer than I should. I was excited by this meeting of hands. Just his hand and mine in one clasp.

'What's wrong? You are simply glowing,' exclaimed the nosy Mrs. Moustafa when I met her half an hour later at the tea break. I said nothing; but before I finally left the building at the end of the afternoon when the conference ended, I searched for him in the crowd. He stood alone in a far corner near an open window. 'I came to say good bye,' I said somewhat hurriedly, trying to sound matter-of-fact. 'It was good teaching here,' I added.

'It is generous of you to say that. You were very professional.'

'I wouldn't say that.'

'What would you say?'

'I was trying to do the best I could.' I put out my hands and he became confused. 'Well good bye, Surin,' I said.

'Good bye,' he replied. We both stood and looked awkward facing each other as our shadows grew; and then I turned and moved rapidly away for I found that I had a desire to embrace him gently and be embraced in turn. As I hurried down the steps a feeling of sadness came over me, and I became aware that there were deep feelings within me that had not been fully

181

bridled by my culture or my upbringing. How did that come about? Had I not been fasting during feast days since the age of four and so knew what restraint was? Had I not been told numerous stories about self-discipline and self-denial by my mother?

I walked home bathed in the last dying glow of a tropical dusk, feeling that I had already moved far in my relationship with young men. There was a time when I would have been uncomfortable, sitting on the school bus, if the hem of my skirt had as much as touched the bare knee of a fellow student. School buses were always a tight squeeze and, to my disapproval, many romances started there. Yet here I was deeply moved by friendship and filled with affection for someone I really didn't know. For the first time I saw how easy it was to drift into falling in love. I told myself that I must be on my guard lest my tender feelings overcame my reason.

I came from a culture of arranged marriages and a family I trusted. I had faith in my father, as did so many others, for he was filled with much good commonsense and I did not believe him capable of arranging anything that would not succeed. It was true I only knew of successful marriages and that the husbands and wives of unsuccessful ones kept their pain and daily frustrations under a strong cloak of duty and responsibility towards their children. At no time therefore did I have a fear or dread of arranged marriages. I could see that marriages needed the beautiful cohesion of tender feelings; yet I had noticed that where the wife could neither sew nor cook nor manage a home; and where her husband did not earn much, such marriages rarely developed into anything splendid, comforting and worthwhile. And there was poor Renee, abandoned by the father of her children, her short life harnessed to a cartful of burdens as she trudged on alone.

One year out of school and we had been transformed, from schoolgirls into young working women. The three girls I knew well had left. Two had gone to India to study English and one to England to study French. I had been to their going-away parties, eaten the food and talked of the old school and of the mannerisms of friends and teachers. We laughed and behaved in a way that said we had lost some of the close tribal ties of the school uniform. We did not know then, in the midst of our jollity, that this would be the last time we were going to be together recalling a common experience. I had been to Port of Spain wharf to see them off and had waved goodbye until their faces blurred and the dark expanse of water between us looked ominous.

Several times in July I had telephoned the Ministry of Education only to be told that they had not yet heard. By the second week of August I began to feel ill at ease. All the misgivings I had kept to myself came to the fore. I discussed the matter with my father and with the help of a family friend made an appointment to see the Assistant Director of the Ministry of Education.

It was an old green wooden building with old-fashioned green jalousies. I had come too early; no one was there but the cleaning lady. She was dusting the stairs with a handbrush.

'You early, man,' she said. 'What's the time?'

'Quarter to nine.'

'By a quarter to ten things really get going. Anyway you will know next time.'

'I have an appointment with Mr. Mohammed; you know which room is his?'

'Who is he? A tall fellow with glasses?'

'I don't know.'

'Well if is he, it's upstairs. Ask anyone. You will find somebody upstairs who can help you.'

'Thank you.'

'That's alright, man. What you think the good Lord send us down here for if is not to help one another?'

As the morning sun rose higher a number of civil servants went upstairs and after a while I decided to follow their steps.

Opposite the stairs a room with a bar door faced me. I pushed it and, as I entered, the door swung back with unexpected speed, making such a commotion that heads looked up from desks to see my entrance.

There were desks all around the walls of the room and down the middle. There were shelves packed high with files from top to bottom; even beneath the large bottom shelf, files were stacked. They looked so tightly packed that any attempt to remove one threatened an avalanche. They were curling at the edges and some bulged so much that they had to be held together with rubber bands.

I stood at the entrance, unsure which desk to approach.

'Can I help you?' a Chinese lady asked.

'Good morning, I am not sure where to go. I have an appointment with Mr. Mohammed for 9.15.'

'What's it about?'

'I haven't heard yet from the university.'

'When did you apply?'

'Last year for this year.'

'Well it is August; you should certainly have heard by now. What name is it?'

'Kamla Maharaj.'

'I will tell Mrs. Griffith that you are here. Take a seat.'

The Chinese lady returned and said, 'Mr. Mohammed will be seeing you shortly; you may sit in Mrs. Griffith's office in the meantime.

After fifteen minutes I began to get restless. I did not want to get in anyone's 'bad books' but this entire business, this long waiting, the many telephone calls, the dry civil servant courtesy of, 'Sorry we haven't heard yet', had made me tired and angry.

'It is now a quarter to ten, and I had an appointment for nine fifteen,' I said.

Mrs. Griffith stopped typing, looked around as if negotiating with something unseen, pushed her chair back, sighed, but then got up and knocked on Mr. Mohammed's door.

I was willing to bear the consequences of my complaint, though it was clear Mrs. Griffith felt I ought to be grateful for his agreeing to see me.

Mrs. Griffith came out and said, 'Mr. Mohammed will see you now.'

I cautiously entered the half-opened door, not knowing whether I should knock. I decided to play safe.

Mr. Mohammed was behind an enormous desk and on the telephone. He smiled and gestured me to sit in one of the three chairs before him. I looked around the room and tried not to listen to what he was saying.

I was studying the layout of the room when he put down the telephone and said, 'Yes, tell me.'

'Last year I applied to Exeter University to study Geography and now that there is only one more month before universities open. I am very worried that I haven't heard.'

'Yes, you should have heard. I want to look at your file to see what the problem is. You should certainly have heard by now. If you would sit with Mrs. Griffith – when she brings in your file I'll call you.'

After another twenty minutes of harrowing silence, I went over in my mind how I had filled out the form, how I'd made sure that I kept to a straight line by the use of almost invisible pencil markings, how because of my anxiety I'd had to rest my moist hand on blotting paper as I wrote, and how, after checking and double-checking every question and answer, I had travelled from Tunapuna to Hayes Street in Port of Spain to hand in my application in person, not trusting the post to deliver something so important.

Mrs. Griffith picked up the telephone and said, 'Are you sure?' There was a pause and then, 'I see... hmmmmm.' She moved slowly into Mr. Mohammed's room as if her task had become weightier, and closed the door behind her. Several minutes later she came out and said, 'Mr. Mohammed will see you.'

'Sit down,' he said. 'I have bad news for you.'

I knew that my Higher School Certificate results were not as good as I had hoped, but because of this I had opted for a university with a good Geography Department, but not widely known. Besides, I knew that girls with similar results had already got university places.

But his words brought into the open my secret fears. My stomach wanted to escape and my lungs to follow.

'They can't find your file I'm afraid. They had a thorough look but it cannot be found. It is as if it never existed, no trace of it.'

'It doesn't make sense. I filled in the form and brought it in here myself. I brought it in early because I didn't want to be a last minute applicant.'

'Oh, I am not saying you didn't. They just can't find it. Just one of those things.'

'Well,' I thought, 'what negligence and all he can say is "just one of those things".' My whole career – just one of those things. What do I do now? I should have sent it by post. All that extra effort and to no avail. Each file is someone's future; why don't they see it like that? Just disappeared? I can't believe it. What can I do?' I knew I couldn't return to school to try and improve my grades. School provided no second chance. And it was too late to apply for the better teaching jobs. I knew that I had handed my file a year ago to a civil servant in this building. Why hadn't I taken his name? What did he look like? What could happen to a file? But I knew that even if they were to find it, it would be of little use to me now. Silence pervaded the room; I felt alone. It was so unreal.

'I am sorry about this,' he broke the silence.

Tears began to flood my eyes and I bent my head. I remembered handing in my large brown envelope and feeling good on my way back from Hayes Street. It was a long journey and a long walk from the taxi stand in Henry Street and back, but I had so wanted to make sure. 'The early bird catches the worm,' Mr. Skinner had said so many times.

I remembered the farewell speeches made at school and the going-away presents, the thoughtful trifles handed to me by children in my class with 'bon voyage' and 'good luck' written in an uneven hand. Could I go back? What would I say? Could

I face another year of nature study? What would I tell my mother, she who had so much faith in the world? What would she make of such incompetence?

I said, 'What can I do now? I've already resigned my job.'

'We're looking to see whether there are any universities in the U.K. with late closing application dates.'

'Thank you.'

'Dear God,' I thought, 'let there be one.' I looked around. The large desk, the walls, the electric bulb, the files, the shelves. They all seemed to be looking at me. I felt lonely and oppressed in the indifferent hush, the shhhhhh of the room.

Am I doing the right thing? Is this a headache I'm getting? Should go outside for a while. Hemmed in. Better outside, so cramped here. Get in the sun, feel the air. If I leave what will they think? That clock; is that all? One minute? I sit alone in Mrs. Griffith's room. Waiting. Waiting. That shhhhhh again; it fills the room.

'Come in, Miss Maharaj,' Mrs. Griffith says; her face reveals nothing.

'We have found one, I am pleased to say. It is Queen's University in Belfast, in Ireland. Its closing date is 19th September.'

'Does the Government recognise this university?' I ask.

'Yes, it is in the North and the North is British.'

'Do they have a Geography Department?'

'Oh yes. A good one too by what they are offering.'

'May I have a look?'

The page is smooth and thin; in a sea of white, thick islands of paragraphs float in my vision. Climatology, Economic, Surveying, Historical, Human, Political, Regions, General, Honours, Archaeology: words that don't make any connection. I see the capital letters. Nothing makes sense, but I have to decide now. What am I looking for? What is a good department? How can I tell from this thin white page with its fine print? Order? Everything is well laid out. Official-looking.

'Well, what do you think?'

'It is difficult to say but it looks alright.'

'Well, would you like to apply?'

I was given an application form and led to a table. My emotions were mixed. I felt a deep frustration as I started to fill out my name, beginning again, starting once more from scratch at this twelfth hour. At the same time I was thankful to Mr. Mohammed for trying.

This time I was not so meticulous in filling out the form. There was no longer something special about it. Even so I checked and double-checked everything to make sure there would be no further delays caused by any omission on my part.

I handed in the form and Mr. Mohammed assured me they would send it off straightaway and that it would get there before the deadline. The deadline was 19th of September. It was then the 19th of August.

When I told my mother she accepted it all stoically. 'Who knows, maybe you were not meant to go to Exeter. You should go to the *siwala*.'

I went to the temple everyday, early in the morning as my mother had suggested. After two weeks I began to look at the postman with special interest.

At the end of the third week, after three weeks of daily prayer, there were times when I could feel quite detached about it. I could apply to teach in another school and then, next year, with more savings, I could go to one of the recognised universities in Canada.

But at other times the days dragged in the humid August and September heat and I felt that I could not spend another year in this listless way, without drive, without working towards something bigger than myself. And so, on my own, I made applications to three of the government recognised Canadian universities. I had to do something rather than just wait.

One month from the day of my application, on the 19th of September, I received a letter from Queen's University accepting me. Registration was on October 4th. I had two weeks to get to Belfast.

I was happy and relieved and told my mother who listened calmly. I knew she was praying that what was best for me should happen, but at the time I don't think I fully realised what this would mean for her. I was the one who accompanied her to the cinema and to Mount St. Benedict. It was I who sat in the shop with her, chatting about the people around us. It was I to whom she had told so many stories from the *Ramayana*. It was I she took to the Port of Spain shops when she was keen to ensure the fine quality of clothing fabric.

But she never said that she would miss me. She was happy for me, pleased that I was going to better myself, she who had never been sent to school, who was self taught.

Now I had only two weeks to prepare myself and get to Belfast in time for registration. It was now out of the question to go by sea, as all my friends had done. I had romanticised the journey by ship with its large dining room and small friendly tables, the chats and games on deck, with time for reading and reflection. It would have been a gradual approach to so much I didn't know. Was fog really like that – was it as I had seen it at the beginning of the film *The Tale of Two Cities,* so mysterious and ghostly? Now if I travelled by sea I would arrive two weeks late for lectures and might not find suitable accommodation; in 1957 Queen's University had no halls of residence for female students. I would be on my own. How would I manage, weeks late, in a quiet university town without adequate provision for students? It was clear that I would have to fly.

I went into Port of Spain and found that air travel was twice as expensive as sea travel. My father had known this but I was hoping that the discrepancy would not be so large. I feared the consequences of the extra expenditure on him. He was suffering from diabetes and had my brother to support through medical school, and I knew that he worried that our clerks were honest stewards only in our presence.

Once more my anger rose at the civil servant who was responsible for losing my file. The burden on my father saddened me and I wished I had the courage to take the passenger liner, arrive late and yet manage well.

Eventually the girl at the desk came up with the least expensive air fare to Belfast. It was still substantially more than the sea fare and entailed travelling to New York, overnighting there and then taking a plane to Shannon in Ireland. From there I had to change planes for Dublin and from there take a train to Belfast. I decided to go that way.

The British Council in Belfast had to be informed of my arrival time. And I had to begin to think afresh of what I would need, not in terms of a trunk as previously, but in terms of one suitcase. I had to leave in less than a week's time.

LEAVING HOME

The dress I wore was beautiful, soft and comforting; it was lined with pink satin and a warm pink glow came through the white sheen of the flowered material. It was an empire line – to give my five foot four some extra height – with tiny covered buttons, sleeveless, the neckline high and rectangular, very chic, accompanied by a matching long-sleeved jacket with a Chinese collar – Mandarin elegance! I was slender and I walked tall.

Mrs. Miller, our family seamstress, fastidious and very neat in appearance, had made it for me.

'Don't hold in your waist now,' she had said, as she took the measurements. 'I've never been on a plane but I heard that your feet does swell up, so don't take off your shoes. You wearing new shoes?'

'Yes.'

'What colour?'

'White.'

'Pink would be much better. I don't fancy white myself. Too ordinary. This is a special occasion – a once-in-a-lifetime thing. Wouldn't you say that, Maharajin?'

'She said she wanted white, so she can use it with other things,' said my mother.

'Well alright then. As I was saying, I will give you about half an inch ...mmmm... a half inch leeway, Maharajin, is that all right?' My mother said nothing, but her face showed it was a silence of agreement.

There was a time when my mother sewed all our dresses, her own and her mother-in-law's, as well as embroider all our pillowcases on the foot sewing machine. But as time passed she found she was not threading the machine as easily as she once did. She got a pair of glasses. More time passed and she said that her head was not good for sewing any more. No one believed her, especially as she continued to sew everything except what she considered special. This dress was special. I was going to wear it on the day I left Trinidad for a faraway country, meeting people we did not know.

Mrs. Miller, fully aware that she was speaking to a fellow seamstress, needed to have her approval.

'A half inch all round then? Just in case the body expands eh? Better safe than sorry. Isn't that true, Maharajin?'

When the day arrived, the moment for my departure from my village, from my home and from my family, I had strange mixed feelings. I was hot one minute and cold the next, and my stomach seemed empty of everything but air. Never before had a female, either on my mother's or my father's side of the family, had the opportunity to go to university – furthermore a university four thousand miles away where there was neither family nor friend.

I knew nothing of Northern Ireland but I was wary of England where I would spend the long summer vacations. It was the place from which Shakespeare, Milton, Shelley and Keats and Wordsworth came. But it had also produced Elizabeth I who had knighted Englishmen like Sir John Hawkins who had got rich through buying and selling slaves. It was also the England that had brought my great-grandparents from India under forced and oppressive circumstances. I had read and enjoyed Jane Austen's *Pride and Prejudice* and *Emma* and Dickens' *Nicholas Nickleby,* Charlotte Bronte's *Jane Eyre, East Lynne* by Mrs. Henry Wood and several memorable pieces and extracts from English literature. What would I make of such a place? It seemed such a mixture of barbarism and sensitivity, of deep insights and callous indifference. I was excited and afraid.

I was, as my father put it, 'to attend the highest institutions of learning'. The way he spoke, you felt the universities were like temples, places to be revered, where the goal was truth and a better understanding of our world. It was a place for serious thought and work. I began to wonder whether I was up to it; whether I would be able to pass my examinations. And there was the suddenness of it all. Most of the intense anxiety and disappointment was now behind me. But some sadness lingered within. I was deeply concerned about my father who of late looked so frail and quiet.

The clothes I was wearing for this journey were more suitable for a cocktail party than travel, but to most people, going abroad was like going to a very special party. But there was a built-in assumption, never questioned, that going abroad by its very nature meant a transformation of self, a dramatic improvement of one's status. One would join the professional classes, or become rich with fairytale speed.

My mother and elder sister had made most of my travel arrangements. They did all that it is possible for one person to do for another and more. They neatly packed my suitcase in stages throughout the week, each day adding something, and then sometimes deciding that I might not need it. From time to time my sister would call me to show where she had placed certain garments, so that I would find them with ease. When it was open, my clothes came about one foot above the rim of the suitcase, and one person had to sit first on one end and then on the other, before it could be closed.

I was wearing beautiful stockings, patterned with sequins above the heel and new court shoes. My sister Maya had dressed my hair in a classical Indian style. It felt firm and steady. I knew that never again would it look so neat and elegant.

An air of restless excitement was everywhere in our home. It could not be contained and it overflowed into the yard and the road in front of the house. Friends of my parents came to wish me well and say how glad they were that I was going to improve myself, that I should try not to forget them in the village. The night before, old friends of the family who had seen me grow, from creeping about in the yard to riding my bicycle, were overcome by my leaving them and by what they called the meaning of my going: the sacredness of knowledge and learning and the acquiring of skills by women; these were good things. They themselves hadn't had the opportunity, but they were too happy to have lived to see this day, when a Hindu girl from this village was going to England. (England was the only place we spoke about: Scotland, Wales and Northern Ireland were encompassed by that word.)

When my father's eldest sister came, she greeted me with a warm hug and a kiss, dried her eyes and said I was looking very good, that she was praying that all would go well and would continue to pray until I arrived at my final destination. She added: 'Who would have thought of a day like this when our grandmothers and great grandmothers left India, not knowing where they were going? All they were told was that there would be work. They came in good faith; they placed themselves in God's hands. And look at this now, look at this success story.' She was smiling. 'Your father can today finance not only his son but also a daughter. What do you call that?' And she beamed with so much pride and so much happiness, I felt humble and so inadequate. She continued:

'Do you know what my grandmother said? She was a little girl at the time, of course. She said there was nothing, nothing at all to see, only water; turn this way, turn that way, nothing else but water for six slow months. And how do you think they were treated? What do you think they were given to eat? She was frightened you know, but she trusted in God and she kept all those doubts to herself. But all that is behind us now. We are healthy and God has blessed us and He has also blessed our children. Thank God.'

Others talked about how different travel was now – the days of six months from India were over; of how bad it had been in the old ships and how many had died. Things had changed for the better; they were so happy for me. Still others said they did not know whether they would live to see me return. They hugged me; a few old neighbours wiped their eyes with their *orhnis* and I too felt a heaviness within and was thoroughly overcome by all this goodwill towards me by people of my parents' and grandmother's generation.

But time was moving on, and my uncles, aunts, my grand-mother and first cousins had already taken their seats in their cars, waiting for me to descend the terrazzo stairs. (In 1956 my father had built a grand new two-storey house with fashion-able, highly polished terrazzo steps.) I was about to come down when my mother called me to the bedroom. She placed her hands upon me as I bowed, and blessed me and asked God to be with me at all times. 'Into thy hands I place my daughter,' she said in Hindi. She asked me to remain where I was and called out to my father, who was downstairs chatting with well-wishers.

And again before my father, I bent down with hands clasped as in prayer, touched his feet with the tips of my fingers, and drew them back to touch my forehead. This I did twice. What the full traditional significance of this gesture is, I cannot say, but for me I was acknowledging in private the thousand and one good things my parents had lovingly be-stowed upon me and even now were offering me, a female child, disadvantaged by custom – an untold of freedom and privilege – at much personal sacrifice to themselves. They were sweeping aside time-honoured ways of thinking of their own volition. One human spirit hailing another in an old fashioned way: that is what this gesture meant to me. My father placed both his hands on my head and blessed me. I left the room but he stayed behind for a few quiet moments of prayer. When he came out he looked at his watch and said, 'It's time we make a move.'

'Alright Pa.' I answered and gingerly descended the wet and recently polished terrazzo stairs in my new high-heeled white court shoes. I held on to the terrazzo railings; the thought of slipping and sliding dominated my uneasy tread. My stomach was churning away. I felt hot and uneasy. My mother noticed and called out to our new housemaid to mop the steps dry.

The morning sun had already begun to beat upon the land, and my delay in coming down meant that those who had gone to their cars earlier were now standing about, fanning themselves. I entered the car awaiting us. Only my mother and father accompanied me in that car. Just as the chauffeur was about to pull out of the yard, my mother said to him, 'Wait a minute please. Kamla, just check and see that you have everything – your passport, banker's draft, plane ticket.'

Our car was allowed to lead the motorcade of five cars, and as I sat in the back seat with my mother, my father's thinness and his private battle with diabetes again weighed upon me. Both my parents seemed to have grown older, more vulnerable; becoming frail, quietly and gently. Yet they carried with them an abiding courage only perceived with time. I thought of their childhoods and wondered whether they ever had the luxury of play. Youth they did not experience, for they were always adults – children with the responsibility of adults – making life's weighty decisions from as far back as they could remember; working side by side with their parents. My mother had married at fourteen and my father at sixteen.

As I looked through the window at the fields of long grass and sugar cane, as the car sped towards Piarco Airport along the Churchill-Roosevelt Highway, the magic of my present position struck me again. How come I was going abroad to study? To study! What a grand concept! What luxury! To study glaciers and winds and cities and the whys of things and their distribution and classification. How was it my father was able to make this possible? He would have said it was because he was a businessman, I'm sure. But that could only be part of the answer. What of the thinking, the larger vision underlying his decision to leave teaching, to leave his village where there was neither persecution nor starvation, to decide to go to another place, where he would absorb the risks and gradually expand. Those large, life-prospering decisions he made at the age of fourteen. I heard my father's voice moving outwards from our sunny porch: 'I was a pupil teacher in my own primary school – the Canadian Mission Indian school. It was my first job. Each morning I had to call at every home and gather the village children on my way to school. As I walked, my numbers grew for I was like the village pied piper. I had no choice but to take my class to school, for no class meant no school and no pay. My salary was not enough to keep me looking like a teacher – long-sleeved white sea-island cotton shirt, dark trousers, black tie, leather shoes, matching socks and a hat. At the end of two terms I gave my mother my salary to help pay for my teacher's outfit and I returned to the grocery business, where what I wore was immaterial. After a while I looked around me and saw that the village would always remain poor. There was no place to expand. The land was on a terrace, the soil was thin. I decided I would have to go.'

My mother said, 'We made that in good time.' The chauffeur agreed. 'Good going for this time of the day I can tell you.' We had arrived at the airport and everything was moving too quickly with a momentum of its own. My whole family came to help me check in, so we quickly formed a longish queue. When we left the check-in counter, my father again looked at his watch and told me that I should now pay my last respects to everyone, starting with my uncles and their wives. I had not quite made the round when passengers for Pan American flight 101 to New York were being called. I hurriedly tried to kiss as many as I could without rumpling my sister's handiwork on my hair, kept in place by numerous invisible hairpins and clips.

I got into line with the other passengers. My sister Maya handed me my new travelling bag with its few articles of clothing, to prevent me from having to open that suitcase during my overnight stay in New York. When I reached the top of the stairs to the aircraft, I turned round and waved, smiling broadly in the direction of my family group. The air hostess said impatiently, 'Come along now.' I was entering a world where time had a far greater significance than I was used to and where, as I learnt, it was weighed and sold on a finer scale.

The hostess showed me to a window seat and helped with my seat belt. I looked around and located an arrow pointing to that essential place as we slowly began to move up the air strip. I peered through the window to locate my family, and though I saw a crowd of well-wishers waving to the aircraft, their faces were too distant to be recognisable; but I knew my father and mother and grandmother and Daya and Maya and all the others would be waving goodbye, so I waved too, while the aircraft moved at such a speed, cutting through the wind, grumbling loudly. It heaved and shook and I knew we were airborne for I felt a dreadful lightness in my stomach.

Sitting there I could hardly believe that a month ago I had no university to receive me and had been so despondent. What awaited me I hadn't a clue. Would I be able to manage the work? As I became more at ease thousands of feet high, scenes of my childhood appeared before me and I began to wonder which persons, what situations, what combination of things, of place and of time, had come together and made me what I was. And suddenly the pain of knowing that I would not be seeing my parents for three years gushed out. Within the aircraft everyone was silent and I could hear its droning noise. I was going to an unknown place; I had made up my mind so quickly, too quickly. Why? My cheeks were moist and I had a heartfelt wish to be sitting in the long grass beside the brook talking to the fishes.

achar: a spiced, hot pickle.

aloo: potato.

angochar: a scarf, usually worn by a pandit.

arati: a ceremony performed in adoration of a deity, by a circular clockwise movement of a lighted lamp or burning camphor.

avatar: an incarnation of a Hindu deity, especially Vishnu, usually in human form.

baigan: melongene, egg plant, aubergine.

bara: fritters made of split-pea flour and spices.

bodi: a long succulent bean.

chatni: a cold relish, for instance made of green mangoes.

chennet: a tropical fruit resembling a lychee in size and appearance when opened.

chulha: an earthen fireside or oven.

dahi: yoghurt.

dhoti: loin cloth.

dia: small earthen bowl used as an oil lamp at prayers, particularly at *diwali,* the festival of light.

ground provision: tropical root crops. e.g. sweet potatoes, yams, dasheen, cassava, eddoes.

gulabjamun: a small thin doughnut, dipped in syrup or rose-water.

jhandi: a flag, usually triangular in shape, erected outside Hindu homes after the holding of *puja.*

jharay: to brush someone with a bundle of leaves, usually *neem* (basil), whilst uttering *mantras* (prayers) to cure them of some ill.

jilebi: a sweet, spiral-like, usually orange-coloured snack made from a batter of yeast and cake flour, deep-fried in oil and dipped in syrup.

kachourie: spicy fritters made from chickpea flour and green onions.

katha: a religious gathering at which stories from the Hindu scriptures are usually told. Usually a bigger ceremony than a *puja.*

keraila: a bitter edible gourd.

kheer: a sweetened, creamy and rich dish of rice and milk.

kurta: a long, usually collarless tunic worn by men.

kutchala: an Indian condiment.

ladu: a soft round sweetmeat, made of sugar, ghee and flour.

machan: a high table made of bamboo to give running vines a platform.

maba: a garland.

pahgree: turban.

peerha: a low bench, usually about six inches high.

pehnoose: sweetened curd.

pehra: an Indian sweetmeat.

pholourie: savoury fritters made of chickpea flour.

pone: a cake or pudding made from cassava or corn.

puja: a prayer ceremony, often held at home.

sadhu: a pandit's assistant.

sadhuayin: a female *sadhu*

siwala: Shivala – Shiva's temple.

soucouyant: in folklore, a woman with the ability to shed her skin, who turns into a ball of fire and sucks her victims' blood at night.

supari: betel nut, a red nut chewed as a mild narcotic.

tharia: a brass plate, often used in religious ceremonies.

tolum: a sweet made from grated coconut and molasses.

vedi: altar.

work house: someone who works in the house and around it all day long; a woman who works all day long.

zabocca: avocado pear.

Lakshmi Persaud was born in Pasea Village, Tunapuna, Trinidad. She studied at Queen's University, Belfast and has taught in Guyana, Trinidad and Barbados. She now lives in London.

Butterfly in the Wind, her first book, was published in 1990.

Her second novel, **Sastra**, published in 1993, is a moving and tender love story, a rich evocation of the Trinidad village world of the 1950s and a memorable portrayal of a brave young woman who has to choose between the traditional, collective Hindu society of her parents and the world of individual destinies and responsibilities. Kenneth Ramchand wrote of 'feeling that you are part of something very abstract and very physically there', and Mervyn Morris praised the 'assurance with which Sastra registers inner turbulence'.

Her most recent novel, **For the Love of My Name**, was published in 2000. It tells, through multiple voices, of the last days of the Caribbean island of Maya before it sinks beneath the sea, the consequence of the weight of its moral corruption and physical neglect. It profoundly dramatises the consequences of ethnic prejudice and of a culture of masks which gives licence to individuals to abandon moral responsibility for their actions. *Caribbean Beat* called it 'an ambitious and important book'.